One of the Boys

One of the Boys

Janet Dailey

G.K. Hall & Co. • Chivers Press
Waterville, Maine USA Bath, England

This Large Print edition is published by G.K. Hall & Co., USA
and by Chivers Press, England.

Published in 2001 in the U.S. by arrangement with
Richard Curtis Associates, Inc.

Published in 2001 in the U.K. by arrangement with
the author.

U.S. Hardcover 0-7838-9119-9 (Romance Series Edition)
U.K. Hardcover 0-7540-4732-6 (Chivers Large Print)

The state flower for New Jersey is the purple violet.

The text of this Large Print edition is unabridged.
Other aspects of the book may vary from the original edition.

Set in 16 pt. Plantin by Myrna S. Raven.

Printed in the United States on permanent paper.

British Library Cataloguing-in-Publication Data available

Library of Congress Cataloging-in-Publication Data

Dailey, Janet.
 One of the boys / Janet Dailey.
  p. cm.
 ISBN 0-7838-9119-9 (lg. print : hc : alk. paper)
 1. Television camera operators — Fiction. 2. New Jersey —
Fiction. 3. Large type books. I. Title.
PS3554.A29 O5 2001
 813´.54—dc21
                                                    00-033500

One of the Boys

Chapter One

Two small round tables were shoved close together in the dimly lighted hotel lounge. There was hardly an inch of surface that wasn't covered with drinks, ashtrays, pretzel dishes and candle-burning globes. Almost a dozen chairs were crowded around the two tables, all of them occupied by men, except one.

Petra Wallis was the sole female in the group, but she was accustomed to that. At five foot nine she was as tall as most of them. Despite her khaki blouse and slacks of a mock-military fashion, there was nothing masculine about her. The very blandness of the unisex-designed clothes accented her slim willowy frame and served as a contrast to the long wheat-blond hair pulled away from her face and secured with a gold clasp at the back crown of her head. The length of it fell straight down her back in a shimmering silk curtain of gold.

Nature had blessed her with a flawless complexion and strong, classical features. Her jawline slanted cleanly to her pointed chin. Her mouth was wide with a sensually full lower lip, her nose straight with the faintest suggestion of an upward tilt at the tip. And her sea-green eyes possessed a naturally thick fringe of dark brown lashes.

Pet, as her co-workers affectionately called her, had often been told she was model material, but she wasn't interested in being in front of the camera. She preferred being behind it.

In the confusion of several conversations and jokes punctuated with laughter, Pet asserted herself with ease. "Have any of you seen the inside of Charlie's van?" Her teasing question was answered by a couple of chuckles while Charlie Sutton, who was sitting across from her, smiled like the Cheshire cat.

"You rode down here with Charlie, didn't you, Pet?" one of the men prompted.

"I did. Although after I climbed in that thing, I wondered whether I was asking for trouble or Charlie was asking for a slap in the face!" Her laughter was a rich, husky sound. "The van looks so innocent on the outside."

"Did you get it all fixed up the way you wanted to, Charlie?" one of the other men asked.

"Almost," he shrugged with a twinkling light in his brown eyes. "There are still a couple of things I want to add."

"I can't think what they'd be!" Pet retorted in an exaggerated reaction, and turned to the others. "He claims he uses it to go camping. It resembles a bachelor's playpen on wheels — silver shag carpeting on the floor, walls and ceiling; a single bed with a black fake-fur spread; a built-in bar," she began describing the inside of it. "The stereo speakers are hidden throughout. A flick of a switch and you have music to make love by. There's even a compact refrigerator to supply ice for the bar drinks!"

"You should have put those mirror tiles on the ceiling, Charlie," someone suggested. "What do the wife and kids think about it, Charlie?" another person teased.

"Sandy loves it," Charlie insisted. "We can slip away for a weekend and have all the comforts of a motel room without the cost."

"It's all prepaid in the money you spent fixing the van," Lon Baxter stated from his chair next to Pet's, and reached for one of the glasses of beer on the table.

"Whoops! That's mine, Lon." Pet rescued her drink and put another glass in his hand. "This is yours."

"How can you tell?" He looked skeptically at the half-empty glass of beer she had substituted for the fuller one.

"Unless you've started wearing lipstick, this has to be mine." She laughingly showed him the peach-colored imprint on the rim of the glass.

"In this light I don't see how you can see anything." He groped in mock blindness, pretending to discover the bareness of her forearm. "Ah, what's this?" Setting his glass down, he took advantage of the fact that Pet was still holding hers. He turned in his chair to get closer to her while his other hand slid across her stomach, stopping on her rib cage just below the swelling curve of a breast.

"It may be dark, Lon," Pet smiled sweetly, "but I know exactly where your hands are. And if your left hand moves one more inch, you're going to get an elbow in the throat."

The warning was issued with deliberate casualness, but it was no less sincere because of it. Conscious of the others observing this little byplay, she knew she had to put Lon firmly in his place without making an issue of it.

Lon Baxter was one of the few single men in the camera crew. Young and good-looking, he made passes at anything in skirts, certain he was irresistible to women. Admittedly, Pet found him attractive, but she had learned a long time ago that if she wanted the respect of her fellow workers, she had to stay clear of any romantic entanglements with them.

Lon she probably would have avoided under any circumstances, since she doubted he had a faithful bone in his body, but there had been a couple of men she wouldn't have minded dating. She had tried mixing her social life with work a couple of times, but the involvement invariably caused friction on the job, so since then she had made it a rule to date only men who were outside the television industry.

With an exaggerated sigh of regret Lon withdrew his hand and sat back in his chair, reaching for his beer. His retreat was noted by the others with a few taunting chuckles.

"Shot down again, huh, Lon?" somebody teased.

"Ah, but I'm alive to pursue her another day," he winked. Pet hadn't believed for one minute that he had given up.

"Why don't you put the poor guy out of his misery, Pet, and let him catch you once?" Charlie suggested, knowing exactly what her opinion of Lon Baxter was.

"I know what my competition is going to be in these next couple of weeks," she replied, not taking offense at the ribbing. "I'm not in the class of Ruby Gale, singer turned sex goddess. Lon won't even notice me after he's spent a day looking at her through his camera."

"Ruby Gale, the new Jersey Lily." Andy Turner, the fourth cameraman in the production crew, lifted his glass in an acidly cynical toast to the star of the television special they had come to tape.

Pet, Charlie, Andy, and Lon made up the team of four cameramen. She loathed the tag "cameraperson." The term seemed unnatural and a needless attempt to differentiate her sex, but she usually had to endure the label.

"She is fantastic!" One of the sound technicians spoke up in the singing star's defense. "Do you suppose she'd mind if I asked for her autograph? My wife and I have every one of her albums."

"I wouldn't ask her for anything until the special is all done," Andy advised. "She can be a royal bitch."

"You've worked with her before, haven't

11

you?" someone asked.

"On an awards special a couple years ago," he admitted. "All she had was one song and an award to present, maybe five minutes of the entire show, but her incessant demands created total chaos. I've seen my share of temperamental performers, but Ruby Gale is the worst! This isn't any picnic we're on."

"Dane can handle her," a lighting technician insisted.

A grimness pulled at the corners of Pet's mouth. "Dane Kingston, the big man himself, is going to be here. I understand this production is going to carry his personal stamp as both producer and director."

"I thought Sid Lawrence was the director," one of the gaffers questioned her statement.

"He's just the assistant director," Andy retorted. "When you're Ruby Gale, you can demand number one and get it."

"Dane is probably going to be on hand to protect his investment," Charlie suggested. "After all, this special is costing him a hefty chunk of dough. I'll bet he wants to be sure it stays within the budget."

"And I'll bet he makes a hefty chunk of dough out of it," someone remarked enviously from the adjoining table.

"I agree he's here to protect his interests," Pet inserted dryly. "Money as well as Ruby Gale."

"What do you mean?" Joe Wiles, one of the

12

lighting technicians and the grandfather of the group, frowned at her comment.

"Dane Kingston and Ruby Gale are what the gossip columnists describe as a hot item. From all accounts, they're having a very torrid affair." A disdainful kind of sarcasm thinly coated the information Pet relayed. She tapped a cigarette out of the pack lying on the table.

Ever attentive to the female, Lon leaned over to light it for her. "Some say he wined and dined her just to get her to sign to do this special," he remarked.

"She's a highly talented performer, but if she's the bitch you say she is, Andy —" Pet blew out a thin stream of smoke while sliding a look at the sandy-haired cameraman "— then it seems to me that she and Dane Kingston are perfectly mated."

"What do you have against Dane?" Andy laughed. "I wouldn't wish Ruby Gale on my mother-in-law, let alone someone like Dane. Besides, I always thought you women went for him. At least, my wife tells me he's quite a hunk of man. And I've always been convinced that she knows a good thing when she sees it — she did marry me."

The joking boast drew the expected round of guffaws and heckling from the group. The conversation could have easily been shifted to another topic, but the mere mention of Dane Kingston had set Pet's teeth on edge. She knew the tension wouldn't ease until she had talked

13

out some of the animosity seething within, veiling it so the rest of the crew wouldn't guess how deeply it ran.

"I have no doubt Dane Kingston can be charming if he chooses." She tapped a long finger on her burning cigarette to knock off the ashes into the half-filled ashtray on the table.

"Let's hope he uses all his persuasive skills to charm our sexy star into performing without her usual temper tantrums," Andy suggested dryly. "Otherwise we'll be in for a long miserable time."

"Who says we won't with Dane Kingston?" Pet countered in a low, venom-filled voice.

"What did Dane Kingston ever do to you?" Charlie asked, subjecting her to his narrowed scrutiny. "I always heard he was an all-right guy."

"Dane Kingston?" She arched one pale brown eyebrow in mocking question, refusing to join the male admiration society for a member of their own sex.

"Did you have a run-in with him or something?" Charlie frowned.

"Haven't you heard the story about Dane and Pet?" Lon Baxter leaned forward, smiling broadly.

Only a few members of the group made affirmative nods. The rest either shook their heads or admitted their lack of knowledge. Their expressions gleamed with curiosity. All of them who knew Pet were fully aware that she couldn't be pushed around, but she was also easygoing and easy to work with. Since she obviously had some kind of grudge against the producer, Dane Kingston, they were interested to know why.

"I don't remember you ever working on a production directly supervised by Dane," Andy commented.

"I haven't," Pet admitted stiffly.

"No, but you remember that variety series Dane produced last year?" Lon was eager to tell the story. "Pet worked on it. The very last show of the package ran into all sorts of problems, delays. You name it and it went wrong. It was way over budget. There was even some question as to whether it was going to be finished in time to make the air-date deadline. When the word finally filtered up through the ranks and reached Dane, he took action immediately and heads began to roll."

"I remember hearing about that," someone agreed. "He threw out the director and a half a dozen others in charge, and finished the last show himself."

"That's what happened," Lon agreed. "Of course, at the time there were a lot of rumors that he was coming to see what was wrong, but he didn't let anybody know when he would arrive. One minute we were talking about him, and the next minute he was there. It was hot that day, really hot. The air conditioner was broken, wasn't it?" He glanced at

Pet, a little vague on that point.

"It was making too much noise and they had to shut it off," she explained indifferently.

"That's right," he remembered. "Anyway, he walks in and what's the first thing he sees? Our Pet in a pair of white shorts and a sexy red tank top. It was between takes and she was getting lined up for the next shot. Evidently nobody thought to tell Dane that we had a woman on the camera crew, because he immediately assumed she was somebody's girl friend. He lost his temper and began chewing her out — and everyone else around her — for messing around with an expensive piece of equipment. Did you know who he was, Pet?" Lon paused in his story to ask.

"No. And I didn't particularly care," she retorted.

"That's for sure!" he laughed. "Nobody wanted to interrupt him to explain who she was, for fear he'd start yelling at them. So finally Pet just shouted at him to shut up. It got so quiet in that place you could have heard a flea scratch. Then Pet began reciting her résumé and wound up telling him that it was idiots like him who didn't know their rear end from a hole in the ground that were causing all the problems on the show, and suggested that he should take a long hike."

There was laughter, but it was generally subdued. The glances that were directed at her, for the most part, held respect and admiration for the way she had stood up for herself. Yet she was fully aware that her defense had been dictated solely by the instinct of self-preservation. She had felt intimidated, overpowered and dominated by the raging giant who confronted her.

"What was Dane's reaction to that?" Joe Wiles was smiling.

"I thought he was going to knock her on her backside," Lon remembered with an amused shake of his head. "He gave her an ultimatum. Either she collected a week's pay and went down the road, or she changed out of the shorts and top into something more respectable and that reminded him less of a streetwalker."

"What did you do, Pet?" The question came from one of the younger men sitting in the shadows of the other table.

"I'm still working for Kingston Productions, so obviously I changed my clothes." Stiffly, she crushed the cigarette in the ashtray.

"It sounds like an honest mistake to me," Andy remarked after giving the story his thoughtful consideration. "You aren't still mad at Dane because of it?"

Pet had encountered prejudice before and usually dismissed it with a shrug of her shoulders. But Dane Kingston's treatment of her was not something she could forgive and forget.

"Dane Kingston is an autocratic, overbearing brute," she declared.

17

"Pet!" Charlie tried to shush her with a silencing frown.

"No, I'm going to say what I think. I don't like him, I've never liked him and I never will like him," she stated forcefully. "If he was here I'd say it to his face."

"Then maybe you should turn around," an icy voice suggested.

A cold chill ran down her spine. Pet turned her head slowly, her gaze stopping when it found the gold buckle of a belt around the trim waist of the man standing behind her chair. Traveling by inches, her gaze made the long climb up his muscled torso, past the set of huskily built shoulders, beyond the tanned column of his neck and the thinly drawn line of his mouth finally to reach the smoldering brown of his eyes.

Her pulse thundered in her ears, reacting to the male aggression of his presence. Pet's seated position intensified the impression that he was towering over her. Perhaps if she hadn't felt so threatened she would have acknowledged that he was a ruggedly attractive man. His dark hair was thick and full, inclined to curl while seeking its own style and order. The sheer force of his personality was enough to make her erect barriers of defense, rather than be absorbed by him.

"I believe there's an old saying that eavesdroppers never hear good about themselves, Mr. Kingston." Her voice was tight with the

18

effort to oppose him.

The atmosphere around the two tables became so thick a knife could have sliced it. Someone coughed nervously while Lon shifted uneasily in the chair beside Pet. She continued to wage a silent battle of wills with Dane Kingston, refusing to be the first one to lower her gaze, but with each second it was becoming increasingly difficult to meet the iron steadiness of his eyes.

Andy cleared his throat. "Er — why don't you join us for a beer, Mr. Kingston? We can squeeze another chair in here."

"Miss Wallis can give me hers," Dane challenged, a mocking glint in his dark eyes. "I'm sure she's tired by now and ready to get some rest."

"Sorry to disappoint you, but I'm not tired — and I have no intention of giving you my chair," she defied him. "Besides, I haven't finished my beer." She turned to pick up her glass as an excuse to look away from him.

"Here, you can have my chair, Mr. Kingston." Someone down the way started to rise.

"Don't bother, I'm not staying," he refused the offer. "I only came by to remind you that we'll start setting up the equipment at six o'clock tomorrow morning. You'd better be thinking about breaking the party up and getting some sleep."

His statement was met with a few grumbles

and self-pitying moans, but the advice was generally taken good-naturedly. By all but Pet, who felt she was capable of knowing how much sleep she needed without being told when she should go to bed.

"Good night." Dane included everyone in the group. "Don't forget, I expect you to be bright-eyed and bushy-tailed in the morning — or you'll wish you were."

"Right, boss."

"Good night."

The replies crowded on top of each other, drowning themselves out. Relief drifted through Pet now that Dane Kingston's unwelcome presence had been removed. She sipped at her beer, but it had grown flat and tepid.

"I feel as if I'm in a dormitory again, complete with curfew," she griped. "Do you suppose he's going to do a bed check and make sure we're all tucked in for the night?"

"Would you like me to tuck you in, Miss Wallis?" his voice came back to mock her.

She jerked around to find he was only a couple of steps away from the table, clearly close enough to have heard her ill-tempered complaint. She could have screamed in frustration, but managed to restrain her anger.

"No, thank you." She had to grit her teeth when she spoke.

"If you change your mind, let me know," Dane taunted deliberately, but his eyes were cold.

This time Pet watched him walk out of the lounge so she wouldn't put her foot in her mouth again. When she turned back to the table, the others eyed her askance, certain she had taken leave of her senses by being so antagonistic. There was a definite possibility that they were right.

"You're asking for trouble," Charlie murmured the warning.

"He rubs me the wrong way," Pet declared with a discouraged sigh.

"We noticed," was the dry response.

Dane's appearance had the desired effect of breaking up the gathering. After he had left, gradual stirring began. Drinks were finished and cigarettes snubbed out in the ashtrays. Chair legs scraped the floor as they were pushed back to allow their occupants to stand. Although she hated to think she was obeying Dane Kingston's instructions to have an early night, Pet followed along with the group as they left the lounge for their rooms.

"It must be nice to have a room all to yourself, Pet," Charlie remarked. "You don't know how lucky you are. I have to bunk with Andy and he snores like a freight train."

"Wait until you have to share a bathroom with Lou!" Joe laughed. "It takes him an hour to comb his hair in the morning."

At a fork in the hotel corridor, Pet turned to the left while the others started right. "This is where I leave you guys. Good night."

"Where are you going?" Lon stopped, although the others wished her good-night and continued on to their rooms.

"My room is down this way," she explained, dangling the room key she had taken from her shoulder bag.

"How come you're down that way when all the rest of us are down this way?" he frowned.

She lifted her shoulders in an indifferent shrug. "Maybe because I have a single room." The question had crossed her mind when she had arrived, but it hadn't seemed important. It didn't now.

"Good night, Lon." She turned to walk down her corridor, the silken straightness of her long blond hair swinging softly below her shoulder blades.

"Wait a minute, I'll walk with you." He hurried to catch up with her. Nearly the same height as Pet, Lon had the advantage of only an inch. As he curved an arm around her waist, his smile promised all sorts of pleasures.

"I can manage myself, Lon." She firmly removed his hand from her waist. "I don't need to be escorted. I won't get lost."

"I just wanted to be sure you got there safely." He looked affronted that she had taken his interest wrong.

"I'll tuck myself into bed. Good night, Lon," Pet repeated, and let her long legs carry her swiftly away from him.

He paused indecisively before he retreated to

the fork in the corridor. Halfway down the hall, Pet reached her room. She had to wrestle with the doorknob before she could persuade the key to unlock the door.

The single room was small. The bed was a little wider than a single, covered with a quilted spread in a blue-flowered print. There was one blue green chair, the same color as the carpet, and a short built-in dresser with a mirror on the wall behind it. A proportionately small television was bolted to an extension of the dresser. The bathroom was about the only thing that was normal size.

Kicking off her flat shoes, Pet dropped her bag and the room key on the bed, and started to move away. On second thought she reached into her bag to take out the pack of cigarettes and her butane lighter, then walked to the single chair. She turned and sank into the seat in a single fluid motion.

Shaking out a cigarette, she snapped the lighter and held the flame to the tip. She glanced at the television, but didn't bother to turn it on. After exhaling the cigarette smoke, she leaned back in the chair to reflect on the lousy beginning of this production.

If she had kept her mouth shut and resisted the urge to vent her opinion of Dane Kingston, he would never have overheard it. Chances were that he had probably forgotten the hostility of their previous meeting. Now she had resurrected it all again when it had been better off buried.

She didn't like him. But just because she didn't like him, she didn't have to tell him that to his face. If you didn't like people you avoided them — or were civil if you had to be around them. But you didn't declare war, which was virtually what she had done.

A sigh broke from her throat. She was usually such an even-tempered person, patient and in control. So why was it that Dane Kingston had the ability to make her lose her cool — to use an outworn vernacular?

The ashes began to build up on the end of her cigarette. The nearest ashtray was on the dresser. Rising to her feet, Pet walked over to lay the cigarette in the glass container. She opened the dresser drawer where she had put her nightgown after unpacking, and laid it on top.

There wasn't much point in staying up since it was after ten. It would be a long day tomorrow, even if Dane Kingston had reminded her of it. She began unbuttoning her khaki blouse and tugging the hem loose from the waistband of her matching slacks.

A knock at the door stopped her action with only two buttons left to unfasten. "Who is it?" Pet called.

"Dane Kingston," was the muffled reply.

She didn't for one minute believe that it was the producer. Some members of the crew had a weird sense of humor. It was more than likely somebody's idea of a really funny practical joke. Irritation surged through her in a quick rush.

"Oh, go away!" she grumbled.

But the person simply knocked again. She had started to tell him she wasn't in the mood for jokes when she decided it would be much more fun to turn the tables on the gagster.

"I'm coming." She deliberately put an inviting lilt in her voice and discreetly buttoned a couple of buttons, but left the top ones undone to permit a provocative glimpse of the shadowy cleft between her breasts.

She sauntered to the door, not bothering with the safety chain as she turned the knob and pulled the door open. "Have you come to tuck me in, Dane?" she murmured sexily.

But it *was* Dane Kingston standing in the hallway!

Chapter Two

Stunned, Pet held the sultry pose she had unconsciously adopted, one hand on her hip and her forearm resting along the edge of the opened door. His dark gaze made a slow and insolent appraisal of her. It was only when he had finished that she recovered from the shock of finding him at her door. The blood rushed to her head, filling her senses with a hot awareness of the situation.

"I thought you were one of the boys — Lon or Charlie." She was instantly defensive.

"Coming to tuck you in?" He cocked his head to one side, a suggestive glint in the hard brown eyes, but the smile touching his mouth was anything but pleasant or amused.

Anger flared at the gibe. "If that's why you're here, Mr. Kingston, I'm neither amused nor interested!" Pet flashed, and stepped back to slam the door in his face.

But it was stopped short of the frame by a large hand moving swiftly to block it. For a fleeting second Pet leaned her weight against it, but she wasn't any match for his superior physical strength. As soon as she realized how undignified she must look, she straightened to simply block the opening.

"What do you want?" She let her exasperation show.

"I want to talk to you," he stated with a crispness that indicated the subject was not personal.

"You've talked to me. Now please leave. I want to get some sleep." She remembered the buttons and hurriedly began to fasten the strategic pair near her breasts. "As you pointed out, we have to be up early and work long hours tomorrow."

"This will only take a few minutes of your precious time, I promise you." Dane Kingston mocked her sudden show of concern for plenty of rest. "Are you going to invite me in? Or do we have this discussion in the hallway where anyone can overhear?"

The flat of his hand was still resting on the door. Pet guessed it would take only one push of that muscled arm to wrench it out of her hand. He could shove his way into her room if he wanted, and there was very little chance that she could prevent it.

"Aren't you worried that someone will see you come into my room at this hour of the night?" she taunted.

"No one that knows either of us. All the rooms for the crew are down the other corridor." There was a humorless curve to his mouth. "So you needn't worry that your reputation is going to be irretrievably damaged by this visit."

Damn! He made her look so foolish and unadult. "I was more concerned about yours," she retaliated, and spun away from the door, admitting him by moving away.

"What did you come to see me about?" She came quickly back to the point of his visit since she hadn't been able to get rid of him.

"Tonight —" he began, then stopped. "Do you always leave cigarettes burning in the ashtray? Don't you know that's a dangerous habit?" he criticized.

"I only do it when someone knocks on the door. Maybe you would prefer that I answer with a cigarette dangling out of my mouth," she retorted, and walked over to crush it out. "My mother always told me that didn't look ladylike."

"Do you think it looks *ladylike* to be one woman sitting in a bar at a table with a dozen men?" He put biting emphasis on her term.

Pet turned to stare at him, seeing the disgust in his expression. Although she was tall, he still had the height advantage, being easily another six inches taller. It was rare that she had to look so far up to anyone, so it was equally disconcerting to have it be Dane Kingston.

"I don't see that it's any concern of yours." She had managed to recover from her initial amazement.

"It should be a concern to you," he countered.

"I work with those boys," Pet reminded him. "Most of them are married with families. Joe Wiles is a grandfather. Why is it a crime to sit around a table and have a drink with them?"

"Do I have to spell it out to you, Miss Wallis, how out of place you looked sitting among all those men?" His eyes had narrowed to dark brown slits. "Since you appear to have some interest in your reputation, may I suggest that you leave the drinking and the talking to the men?"

Pet was astounded by his suggestion — and angry. "What am I suppose to do on my off hours? Sit alone in my hotel room while the guys are in the bar having a good time? If that's your idea, you'd better think again," she informed him in no uncertain terms. "If I want to have a beer with the boys, I will."

"In case you haven't looked in a mirror lately —" he grabbed her by the elbow and turned her around to face the wall mirror "— you don't happen to be one of the boys!"

But it wasn't her own reflection that her turbulent sea-green eyes saw in the mirror. It was his, standing tall and dark beside her, overpoweringly masculine beside her willow-slim frame and wheat-tan hair. His innate virility aroused raw feelings of femininity in her. Pet tugged her elbow free of his hold and took a quick step away. She was used to feeling strong and independent no matter what man she was with, not weak at the knees.

"So what do you expect me to do — remain cloistered for the next couple of weeks or however long it takes to finish this special?" she demanded. "I'm not a nun! I like to laugh and socialize and — wait a minute!"

She turned on him roundly, a thought suddenly occurring to her. "Is there some significance to the fact that my room is in this corridor while the boys all have rooms in the other one? Was this your idea? Or is it just because this is a single?"

"When the hotel reservations were made, attention was paid to the fact that you are the only female member of the crew outside of wardrobe and makeup," he admitted smoothly. "It didn't seem wise or proper to put an unattached female in a room next door to a couple dozen men."

"Then you're responsible for my being separated from the others," she said, feeling anger rather than appreciation for this thoughtfulness.

"Yes."

"Am I supposed to thank you for this?" Pet challenged. "Do you have any idea how hard I've worked to be accepted by them? To be treated as their equal? Now I'm in a different wing. You're saying I shouldn't socialize with them at all. What's next? Do I eat at a different table?"

"I suppose you wouldn't have objected to sharing a room with 'one of the boys,' " Dane jeered.

"I suppose next you're going to insinuate that I wouldn't be safe if I spent a night in the same room with Joe Wiles. For heaven's sake, he's a grandfather!" Pet went a step further. "He's old enough to be *my* grandfather." She went to brush past him and escape from the narrow path between the bed and the dresser to the wider space near the chair, where there was breathing room. "You certainly don't have a very high opinion of the members of your own sex!"

Dane stopped her, catching her by the arm and whipping her around to face him. Centrifugal force catapulted her against him, the solidness of his brawny frame bringing her to an abrupt halt. The air left her lungs in a rush at the unexpected contact with his body. As she was not a lightweight herself, the impact rocked him slightly. His large hands spanned her waist to steady both of them, the imprint of his fingers burning through the khaki material into her flesh.

Conscious of the masculine power of his thighs and the steel band of muscles flexing in his arms, Pet tried to collect her scattered wits and slip out of this accidental embrace, but her limbs wouldn't respond to the signals her brain sent out. She felt her heart skipping beats in sheer sexual attraction. Her mind reeled from the possibility that she could be physically attracted to the man.

"You're a stunning amazon." His low voice had a harsh edge to it. "Any normal, red-blooded American male — regardless of his age

— would get ideas in his head if he spent a night alone in the same room with you. Don't tell me you aren't aware of that?"

The warmth of his breath fanned her face and hair like an intimate caress. Its potency was drugging. Fighting it, Pet abruptly turned her head to face him and make a retort. But in turning she discovered his head had been bent toward her, and in consequence her lips brushed the angle of his jaw. The resulting sensation was a shivery tingle that ran through her nerve ends, leaving them quivering for more. She twisted out of his arms as if she had been jolted by an electric prod.

"I'm quite aware of it. I didn't mean to imply that I wanted to share a room with one of —" That phrase "one of the boys" was becoming overused. "But I certainly don't think I have to be in an entirely different wing of the hotel from them."

The phone rang, and Pet nearly jumped out of her skin at the sound. Dane, in a purely reflex action, took the one stride necessary to reach the phone on the stand beside her bed and picked up the receiver. He had barely said hello before Pet realized he was answering her phone.

"Give that to me! Who do you think you are, taking my phone calls?" she demanded, and grabbed the phone out of his hand. "Hello?"

"Pet?" It was a very startled and confused Lon Baxter on the other end of the line.

"What's Dane Kingston doing in your room?"

Oh, God, she thought. "He's lecturing me on the moral behavior proper for a young woman. Isn't that a laugh?" She vented her irritation toward the whole situation. "What did you want, Lon?"

"I . . . I wondered if . . . you wanted to join me for breakfast?" He sounded unsure whether he should even ask.

"Sure," Pet agreed with total disregard for everything Dane Kingston had said. "What time do you want to meet? Is five too early? We have to be at the Garden State Arts Center at six."

"Yeah, five o'clock is all right," he agreed with still a trace of uncertainty.

"Good night, Lon," she prompted him to hang up.

"Yeah, good night, Petra," he said absently.

She sighed as she hung up the phone. All the questions Lon hadn't found the nerve to ask tonight would be dumped on her in the morning. She did have an explanation — a true one. Whether Lon would prefer a meatier explanation of his own was another question. Men were such gossips.

Turning, she saw Dane standing at the foot of the bed, watching her, his hands in the side pockets of his pants.

"Problems?" It was a one-word question with no apology for causing them.

"Nothing that I can't handle," Pet replied shortly.

His dark gaze slid to the phone, then back to her. "So you've decided not to take my advice."

"About socializing with the boys? No, I'm not taking it." With space between them she could think more clearly. She realized the way she had been manipulated, always in reaction to his statements and accusations, and she was irritated that she had allowed it to happen.

"You and I have differing viewpoints. In the bar tonight you thought I looked like a tramp sitting with all those men. For me there's safety in numbers. Before you came to my room I wouldn't have dreamed of accepting Lon's invitation to have breakfast with him alone. But I just did because I knew you would disapprove."

"That's a stupid reason." The corners of his mouth were indented with grimness.

"You bet it's a stupid reason!" Pet agreed. "I can't be friendly to just two or three of the guys. If I do, the rest will assume that I go for them, and that destroys the camaraderie I've struggled so hard to achieve. Why did you have to interfere? Nobody asked you to!"

"I don't need permission to interfere. This is my company, and my production. When I bring a crew on location I ultimately become responsible for a portion of the members' private lives — yours included, Miss Wallis," Dane snapped. "I doubted the wisdom of bringing your kind of temptation on location where the men are going to be away from their wives and girlfriends. The very first night I see you sitting in

34

a bar, drinking with the whole lot of them. I have the feeling you're going to be a lot more trouble than you're worth!"

"Now maybe we've come to the heart of the matter." Her temper rose in direct proportion to his cold anger. "It's my job you want. What do you plan to do? Make my life on the set so miserable that I'll quit?"

"If you weren't good at your job, a highly skilled professional, you would have received your walking papers a long time ago," Dane informed her bluntly. "But if you —" he lifted a hand to point a finger at her and jab the air "— cause one ounce of dissension among the crew, if there's one quarrel among the men about you, I'll send you packing so fast you won't know what hit you."

"Then stay out of my personal life and there won't be!" she flared, and began stabbing the air with her finger. "You can dictate to me on the set, Dane Kingston, but don't you dare give me one order outside of work!"

"How many prolonged location shoots have you been on?" he challenged.

"I've been on quite a few two-day and three-day shoots." Which wasn't exactly a direct answer.

"How old are you?" he demanded next.

"Twenty-six." She would be in September, which was only two months away. The extra year implied more experience.

"I top that by eight years. And I've seen happily married men make complete fools of themselves when they've been separated from their wives for a week. Why do you think Miss Gale and her singers and dancers are staying in a different hotel?"

"I . . . presumed it was more luxurious than this one." Pet shrugged a shoulder uncertainly.

"It is. More importantly, it keeps my production crew separated from her cast so there won't be any socializing after hours. If it had been at all practical, you would have been staying in a different hotel, too. Unfortunately, it wasn't." His irritation with that was in his tight-lipped expression. "You just remember what I told you — any trouble and you're out!"

On that threatening note he turned on his heel and let his long, swinging strides carry him to the door. Pet's hands curled into fists.

"You just remember what *I* told *you*," she called after him, trying to assert her own independence, but it was too late. Dane was pulling the door shut behind him as he stepped out into the hall.

Frustrated and dejected, Pet sank onto the squeaking mattress of her bed. She flopped backward to stare at the ceiling and rest the back of her hand on her forehead. This had not been her finest hour, she realized. Nor was the situation likely to improve unless she learned to control her temper around Dane Kingston. He was her boss, for heaven's sake! The *big* boss! You couldn't go any higher in the company than Dane Kingston. Why hadn't she remembered that and behaved accordingly — regardless of the provocation?

Unable to answer that, Pet pushed herself off the bed and walked to the door. She flipped the security lock and the night latch and slipped the chain into place. Perhaps a shower and a good night's rest would put the whole thing in perspective.

The next morning Pet was deliberately late to meet Lon for breakfast. Wearing the same khaki blouse and slacks with their military creases, she had braided her flaxen hair into a single plait down the center of her back. Few women could get away with such a severe style, but Pet could, thanks to her strongly defined features and well-shaped head.

As she had hoped, two members of the crew had joined Lon at his table. She walked to the empty chair. "You saved a place for me. Thanks." The sentence was deliberately chosen to show Lon how casually she had accepted the invitation for breakfast.

"Good morning." She greeted them all as she sat down and felt the curiosity in each of their glances despite the normal chorus of replies. "Is there coffee in the pot?" Pet asked, and reached for the thermal container in the center of the table to pour herself a cup. "I need something to open my eyes this morning."

"Is there enough left for another cup?" Charlie Sutton inquired.

"About a half a cup," Pet answered after glancing inside the pot. The waitress stopped at the table to take her order, Lon and the others having already eaten. "I'm running late, so I'd better settle for toast and orange juice."

"Would you refill the coffeepot?" Joe Wiles handed the empty thermal container to the waitress.

When the girl had left, Pet leaned back in her chair, blowing on the hot coffee to cool it. Over the rim of her cup her gaze swept her three table companions in an encompassing arc around the table. It was early in the morning, but their unnatural silence wasn't caused by sleepiness.

"Come on, guys." She sipped at the hot coffee. "Isn't someone going to ask me what Dane Kingston was doing in my room last night? Or are you going to sit there eaten up with curiosity?" she teased. She had it all thought out, her explanation carefully rehearsed.

"That's our Pet!" Joe Wiles shook his head and smiled wryly. "Straightforward and open."

"You said he lectured you?" Lon looked skeptical.

"Yes. He went off on the same old tangent," she declared with a mock grimace. "Only this time it wasn't about the way I dressed, but what I was doing. He didn't think it was lady-

38

like to have a beer with you guys and he suggested I behave with a little more decorum befitting my sex. Can you imagine?" she laughed, and took another sip of coffee.

"From now on, we'll make sure you order sherry — a proper drink for a proper girl," Joe teased.

"Dane suggested that I shouldn't associate with you at all." Pet blinked her deliberately rounded green eyes. "It seems you boys are a bad influence on an innocent young thing like me." She made it all appear to be a huge joke that everyone could laugh about.

"We *are* a wicked lot." Charlie twirled the end of an imaginary mustache in mock villainy.

"What did you tell Kingston?" Lou's eyes were gleaming with amusement; finally he was accepting her explanation without trying to turn it into something it was not.

"What do you think? I told him to mind his own business!" she declared with a twinkling look.

Her remark drew the expected chuckles and comments that suggested approval and encouragement for her stand. But Pet was careful not to mention Dane's threat about causing trouble or dissension among the crew. For the time being the men were on her side, and she didn't want to put ideas into their heads that might change their attitude.

Claude Rawlins, the floor director, stopped at their table when the waitress brought Pet's toast and orange juice, and the conversation was immediately shifted to a discussion of the day's schedule.

"When we're finished shooting here at the performing-arts center, where do we go?" Pet asked. "As I understand it, the idea is to show Ruby performing in different settings — the concert stage, a casino theater, and so on."

"That's right," Claude nodded. "From here we'll move to Batsto Village for some outdoor locations, then on to Atlantic City to tape her opening night at the casino."

"We're really going to be plugging New Jersey, aren't we?" Lon remarked on a less than enthusiastic note.

"This is her home state. She was born and raised here in New Jersey," Claude reminded them. "These backdrops will all be fresh and new to a viewing audience that's seen Las Vegas casinos and Madison Square Garden or the Kennedy Center hundreds of times."

"I agree," Pet nodded. "I think it's a good idea."

"Spoken like a homegrown Jerseyite," Charlie teased. Which she was.

"Your New York nose is in the air again," she countered.

Joe didn't take part in their playful feud, choosing to stick to the original subject. "It's fitting to tape the special in New Jersey. After all, Ruby Gale has been tagged as the new, American-born Jersey Lily."

"Lillie Langtry was the original Jersey Lily, wasn't she?" Pet remembered. "But she was from England, I thought."

"She was," Claude admitted. "Now we have an American version — if you believe the publicity." He paused to glance at his wristwatch. "You'd better drink your coffee, boys. It's getting late."

Pet quickly downed her last bite of toast and joined the others in line at the cash register. Everyone took it for granted that she would pay for her own meal, including Pet. The situation with the crew seemed to be back to normal.

Eight of them crowded into Charlie's van to make the ride to Telegraph Hill Park where the Garden State Arts Center was located. The early-morning sun cast a golden hue on the saucerlike white building with its supporting pillars. The summer-green setting of grass, trees and bright patches of flowers was serene and pleasing to the eye. Charlie drove around back where the semitrailer van filled with highly technical computers and control panels was parked. Several of the crew had already arrived, and others were driving in behind them.

Dane Kingston had just walked out the side door of the specially designed semitrailer rig and was coming down the set of metal steps shoved against the trailer door when Pet piled out of the van with the others. He noticed her immediately. His hard and narrowed look made her feel she was somehow responsible for their

41

arriving late when in actual fact they were seven minutes early.

But there wasn't time to dwell on the injustice of his attitude. All the camera, lighting and sound equipment had to be set up and checked, which was an involved process. Everyone set to work at once. Pet, Lon, Charlie and Andy Turner entered the center to learn where the cameras would be positioned, and to what position each would be assigned.

In all there were four large studio cameras. One would be kept in reserve in the event of a technical failure of one of the others. Pet was assigned to camera two, covering center stage. Andy was manning camera one on her right and Charlie had camera three on her left. Lon was assigned to the hand-held camera, which allowed him the ability to move around with the lighter-weight camera and provide shots from in back of the stage, from the side, or below the footlights.

The first order of business was erecting the platforms to elevate the fixed studio cameras to a degree higher than stage level. Working as a team, they pitched in to help each other erect the scaffolding for the platforms one at a time. Pet worked right beside the men, not shirking any of the heavier work because she was female.

While they were busy with their work, other members of the production team were busy with theirs. It was a chaos of activity with two dozen people, sometimes more, hustling around, shouting orders amid general conversations. A web of cables was spun over the floor to relay power and feed into the main controls in the long trailer outside.

As soon as the platforms were finished they brought in the studio cameras, disassembled and packed in their metal traveling cases. It wasn't easy for Pet to handle the bulky and heavy pieces, but she had learned little tricks over the years that enabled her to compensate for the lack of muscles. It never occurred to her to ask for help. She would have refused it if it was offered.

"Wallis, what do you think you're doing?" a voice barked behind her.

The suddenness of the demand forced Pet to ease the camera onto the platform floor after she had finally levered it a couple of inches off it. Still kneeling, she turned to look behind her. Dane Kingston was on the floor, glaring at her with his hands on his hips.

He wasn't dressed much differently from any of the other crew, except that his jeans were brushed denim and his shirt was a long-sleeved madras print with the cuffs rolled up to reveal his sun-bronzed and hair-roughened forearms. The modified work clothes emphasized his rugged male appeal, a factor that didn't make Pet feel any more at ease.

His gaze ripped from her to stab Charlie. "Get up there and get that camera mounted,

43

Sutton," he ordered with an impatient wave of his hand.

"I can manage it!" she protested forcefully when Charlie started to vault onto the platform.

"I'm not interested in finding out whether you can or not," Dane retorted, and started to turn away.

"This doesn't happen to be the first camera I've ever assembled. I'm fully capable of doing it alone. I don't need any help," she insisted.

Dane swung back to face her with blazing dark eyes. "You can play superwoman another time. I'm not going to permit you to juggle an expensive piece of equipment like that camera. You'd probably drop it and break it; then I'd be without a spare. I can't afford this kind of idiotic display of sexual equality. You aren't strong enough to lift that camera, so let someone else do it. Do I make myself clear?"

Just in time she remembered to hold her temper, although it flashed in her green eyes. "Very clear, Mr. Kingston," she said, clenching her teeth.

"Good. Make sure I don't have to tell you again," he warned.

He waited at the base of the platform until Pet had moved stiffly out of Charlie's way so he could hoist the camera into place on the rotating head of its stand. As Pet went to help Charlie fasten it into place, Dane walked away. She glared after his set of broad shoulders.

"I've never considered myself superwoman," she muttered angrily. "And I've never asked for special treatment because I'm a woman. Damn him, anyway!"

Charlie's gaze flickered uncertainly over her. "You have to admit, Pet, the camera was a little heavier than you could handle."

"*Et tu, Brute*," she retorted sarcastically, but Charlie didn't hear her as he turned to say something to Andy.

Chapter Three

By midmorning all three of the camera platforms were in place. One of the cameras was
mounted and the crew was unpacking the
second and getting it ready to assemble.

"Break time!" Claude shouted to make himself heard above the racket. "Coffee and sweet
rolls down front!"

"Sweeter words were never said," Pet murmured, and hopped down from the middle
platform. "Those two slices of toast I had for
breakfast disappeared about an hour ago. I'm
starved!"

"Just direct me to the coffee," Andy declared
as he followed her down the aisle. "I must be
eight cups behind my normal quota of caffeine
for the morning, and I was on the verge of getting the shakes."

A long table had been set up near the fire exit
along the wall to the right of the stage. A huge
stainless-steel coffee urn was perched in the
center of it with paper cups stacked on one side
and boxes of Danish pastry on the other. Pet
joined the others who had already lined up to
help themselves.

With her coffee and pineapple pastry in
hand, Pet wandered over to an empty area
below center stage. Andy joined her there.

Soon after Lon and Charlie came and a few of the other crew, to talk shop. Pet listened, but spent most of her time eating to quiet the hunger pains in her stomach. When it was gone, she licked the sticky frosting from her fingers. Tired of standing, but intrigued by a technical explanation Andy was making, Pet set her cup of coffee on top of the stage. With her hands to lever her, she vaulted onto the stage, swinging around to sit on the edge, her long legs dangling. Between sips of her coffee she listened to Andy and asked questions when she wanted something clarified.

She reached for the pack of cigarettes that she usually carried man-fashion in the breast pocket of her blouse. Too late, she remembered they had fallen out when she was assembling the camera.

"Can I bum a cigarette from somebody?" she asked. "I left mine on the platform."

"Here." Lon lighted one of his and handed it to her, the filtered end first.

"Thanks. Coffee without a cigarette is as incomplete as a steak without salt," Pet declared.

"Or a bed without a woman in it!" someone suggested, and everyone laughed in agreement, although Pet just smiled.

"Pet doesn't think so." Lon noticed her silence and began to tease.

"Nope. I have a teddy bear to snuggle up to at night," she joked. "It doesn't complain if I have a headache."

47

"Do you have headaches often?" Charlie asked with a laughing smile.

"Working with you guys, I have them all the time!" she declared with mock seriousness, and drained the Styrofoam cup of its contents.

"Want another cup, Pet?" Andy offered.

"I'd love one," she admitted. "But I can get it."

"I was just going to refill mine. There's no sense in both of us walking over there," he reasoned, and reached for her cup, which she surrendered to him.

"If the queen is through holding court —" Dane appeared at the fringe of the small group, withering Pet with a dry look "— let's get back to work."

A few of the men murmured "Sure," and "You bet," as glances were darted at Pet sitting rigidly on the edge of the stage. Over the heads of her fellow workers her gaze was locked with Dane's. Holding court indeed, she thought angrily. Up until a few minutes ago she had been listening to an impromptu lecture by Andy. And Dane had made it sound as though all the guys had been dancing attendance on her! She was furious, but she held her tongue.

As the group around her began to disperse, it seemed a pathway was being cleared between her and Dane. When he moved to approach her, Pet stayed where she was. The stage gave her a height advantage. She would enjoy looking down on him for a change. No matter

48

what he said to her, she was determined not to lose her temper.

Stopping in front of her, Dane peered at her through spiky male lashes as dark as his eyes. The powerful line of his jaw was hard and unyielding. An awesome mingling of danger and excitement danced along her nerves and she found that she couldn't maintain the silence.

"I wasn't 'holding court,' " she insisted stiffly.

In one smooth motion he came a step closer and spanned her slender waist with his large hands. Instinctively Pet clasped his bare forearms with the intention of repelling his hands, but he was already lifting her off the stage and setting her feet on the few inches of floor left in front of him.

His hands stayed on her waist, as if he knew that the minute he took them away she would move out of his reach. She was forced to stay where she was, their tall bodies almost, but not quite, touching. His nearness was suffocating.

"Don't deny you were the center of attention," Dane stated, a muscle working in his hard jaw.

"Maybe when you walked up, but not before." Her gaze moved restlessly over his shirtfront, looking anywhere but into his implacable male features.

She watched the steady rise and fall of his chest, noticed the curling, golden brown hairs peeping out through the V opening made by an unbuttoned collar, and saw the brawny muscles

49

beneath the shirt sleeves over his upper arms. It was a disturbing observation of his utter masculinity.

"They were clustered around you like bees around honey." His voice was low, but that didn't lessen its cutting edge.

"That isn't true," Pet denied. "They'd gathered around the stage because it gave them something to lean against."

"They leaned against the stage rather than sit in those seats out there," Dane mocked. "In case you haven't noticed, there are several rows of them out there."

"Why don't you quit making mountains out of molehills?" she hissed. "Why do you keep looking for lusting motivations behind a perfectly innocent gathering?"

"Will you listen to me, you long-limbed Nordic witch?" His fingers dug into her waist, inflicting pain. If his intention had been to make Pet finally look at him, he succeeded. "I have a much clearer understanding of the fantasies a man could weave in his head when he looks at you."

"Such as?" Pet challenged, goaded by his superior attitude.

An eyebrow flicked upward in aloof amusement. "Such as wondering whether all your skin would be as marblesmooth and white as your neck if those clothes were taken off you." His downward glance seemed to strip away her blouse and heat her flesh before it finally returned to her whitened face and wide green eyes. "Such as wondering what you'd look like with all that long blond hair flowing freely over your naked breasts." Dane paused. "Do you want me to continue? Because I can, very easily."

"No." Her voice was all choked. She had to swallow to ease the strangling sensation. He had made it sound as if that really was what he thought when he looked at her. For a few seconds she had allowed herself to be carried away by the possibility that he was attracted to her. "Some men might fantasize like that, but not Andy, Charlie or the others. They know me."

"They work with you, but that doesn't mean it never crosses their mind to wonder what you'd be like as a lover. Men tend to think along those lines," he said. "Women probably do, too, but they're reluctant to admit it even to themselves."

"I don't think very many women think like that," she replied huskily.

"No? You've never wondered what it would be like if — for example — I made love to you?" Dane queried, tilting his head to one side.

"No." Pet rejected such a notion with a rushed answer and pushed at his forearms. "Now let me go. I have to get to work. I can't keep standing around here talking to you."

"Or the boys might start to think I was in your room last night for a reason other than the one you told them?" he suggested complacently.

"They wouldn't." But she turned to look toward the middle platform where Charlie and the others had gone to finish assembling the camera. As she watched them, Andy glanced over his shoulder toward the stage. The object of his attention was obviously her and Dane.

"They would enjoy thinking it," Dane insisted dryly.

"Well, I wouldn't!" Angered that he had placed her in another awkward situation, Pet wrenched out of his hands with a violent twist. "So just stay away from me from now on!" With a quick pivot she whirled away from him, her long braid flying out behind her and nearly slapping his face.

Anger gave her a surplus of energy. She burned a portion of it walking up the aisle to the platform and hopping onto the planks. The rest she immediately put to use helping the others, aware of their speculative glances and telling silence.

Finally Andy teased, "Did you quarrel?" She turned on him with a vengeance. "If you think for one minute that I'm interested in that muscle-bound know-it-all tyrant, then you aren't any friend of mine. If he'd been anyone other than Dane Kingston — my boss — I would have told him where to get off! He accused me of holding court. And all because you offered to get my coffee!"

"Are you saying it's my fault?" His look was incredulous. "Only a woman could reason like that."

"Yes, yours! And his —" she waved a hand toward the stage where Dane was talking with the lighting director "— overactive imagination!"

"Do you want us to help you find it?" Lon asked.

Pet turned to glare at him. "Find what?" she demanded.

"You've obviously lost your temper. I thought you might want us to help you look for it," he suggested. The other three were wise enough not to smile in front of her.

"No, thank you. I'll find it myself," she said tightly, realizing that she was unjustly venting her anger on them. "I just need to cool down a little bit."

"Let's speed up the process." Charlie picked up the piece of white cardboard and began fanning her with it.

"Very funny." But there wasn't any amusement in her expression.

She never fully recovered her sense of humor. By the time they broke for lunch, Pet had succeeded in pushing the disturbing incident to the back of her mind. The others had either forgotten or were careful not to bring it up.

In the afternoon, the impression of chaos was increased when the cast of entertainers arrived to practice their songs and dance routines. To an outsider, it had to look as though no one knew what was going on, but it was all very well organized.

Wearing her headset to communicate with the control booth in the semitrailer, Pet was checking out her camera to make certain it was functioning properly and transmitting a clear picture to the monitors in the control booth. Invariably when a sophisticated and sensitive piece of equipment such as this television camera was transported any distance, something needed adjustment. Although generally the adjustments were minor, they could be time-consuming, which was why a day was set aside more or less for the sole purpose of assembling and checking out the equipment, including the spare camera. Barnes was the name of the technician in the control booth with whom Pet and her co-cameramen were working.

"She's here. She just walked in the door." It was Lon's voice that came over Pet's headset. "Wow! She's sexier in person, if that's possible."

"You mean Ruby Gale? Where is she?" Charlie questioned.

Pet had the feeling she was listening in on a party line as the headset hummed with the intercommunication of the cameramen. The star of the television special had arrived and all thought of the technical checklist to be completed had been temporarily forgotten. Admittedly Pet was a little curious to see what Ruby Gale actually looked like in the flesh after having heard and seen her perform so often in the past.

"She's coming down the center aisle," Lon answered Charlie's question.

Turning her head, Pet saw the titian-haired woman skirting the camera platform. Her first thought was how small the star looked, then she realized she was guilty of carrying the larger-than-life screen image in her head. Instead of being as tall as she was, Ruby Gale was probably two inches shorter, but her long shapely legs provided that illusion of extra height.

Glimpses of those famous legs clad in tights were offered by the side splits in her skirt each time she took a step. She had a flaming mass of red hair that cascaded in thick glowing curls around her shoulders. Unfortunately, Pet's only view was of the star's backside as she walked down the aisle toward the stage, so she wasn't able to see if Ruby Gale was as naturally beautiful in the face as she appeared on screen and in photographs. Soon even that view was blocked by the two people who followed closely behind the star, no doubt part of her personal entourage.

Then Pet noticed Dane coming at right angles to intercept the star. A wide lazy smile added a potent charm to a man she regarded as being already too ruggedly appealing. Irritation pressed her lips into a thin line as she watched him greet the redhead with a kiss. In the entertainment business, kissing was as much a part of greeting as a handshake.

"Do you see the way she's cuddling up to Dane?" Charlie murmured. His voice coming over her earphones was an unneeded verification of the scene Pet was witnessing.

"I wish she'd press against me like that," said Lon, and imitated the sound of a growling tiger.

"Dane's certainly enjoying it," Andy observed dryly.

"There would have to be something drastically wrong with him if he didn't," Lon retorted. "Hey, you're awfully quiet, Pet. Isn't there any comment you want to make?"

It took her a second to find her voice. "About what?" With the pencil-thin microphone directly in front of her lips, it didn't take much above a whisper to make herself heard. "She's an absolutely gorgeous woman, but you can't expect me to be turned on about her the way you guys are."

Ruby Gale was very beautiful. Pet could see that now as the redhead half turned toward the audience seats. Her features were sultry and exotic. Her dark eyebrows were perfectly arched, winging to her temple. Full, sensuous lips appeared always silently inviting some forbidden pleasure. Although Pet was too far away actually to see the color of her eyes, she remembered from the photographs of Ruby Gale that they were a startling peacock-blue.

"A word of warning, fellas," Andy inserted. "She has a temper to match the color of her hair."

"I don't care," Lon declared. "All I know is that these next few days it's going to be a treat having to look at her all the time. I'd be willing to pay for the privilege."

"Better not let the union hear you say that," Charlie suggested.

Barnes from the control booth spoke up. "Don't you think we'd better get back to the job at hand, fellas?"

"Joy killer!" Lon grumbled.

Fortunately Ruby Gale disappeared behind stage with Dane and the distraction was eliminated. Not for long, however. Fifteen minutes later she was on stage to rehearse some numbers with the dancers. The skirt and blouse had been discarded in favor of a dancer's leotard and a skintight body shirt that revealed every curve and contour of her breasts. Pet had to suffer through more profuse compliments on the redhead's beauty and well-endowed figure. She was heartily sick of the entire subject when a halt was finally called for the day.

Back at the hotel, Pet showered away her mild irritation and the day's tiredness. The khaki outfit was cast aside in favor of a pair of biscuit-colored slacks and a forest-green blazer over a tan sleeveless top.

She walked alone to the dining room, certain there would be somebody from the crew with whom she could share dinner. There were three tables' worth, with an empty place setting at each table. Pet avoided the one at which Lon and Charlie were sitting since they had been so vocal in their praise of Ruby Gale, and she had already had her fill of that subject.

She proved to be a minority of one. All through dinner every other sentence contained some reference to the star of the television special. It seemed everyone had some anecdote to relate or gossip to add. At the conclusion of her meal, Pet stayed at the table to have coffee with the guys.

When the exodus began toward the lounge, she decided that she couldn't endure another minute of Ruby Gale and opted to return to her room. No one seemed to notice that she wasn't coming with them, which was rather bruising to her ego.

Perhaps that was why she didn't notice Dane Kingston standing near the exit of the restaurant until she was almost level with him. Her steps faltered for a brief instant.

"Good evening," she murmured, and would have walked on.

"Aren't you going into the lounge with the others?" His dark eyes moved over her with lazy knowledge.

"Not tonight. It's been a long day and I'm tired," she explained because she didn't want him to think her decision had been based on his admonition not to socialize with the men in the crew.

"It never crossed my mind that you were heeding my advice," Dane assured her. "But I can't say that you look tired, either."

Pet took a deep breath and released it in an exasperated sigh. "The truth is, Mr. Kingston, that I've become bored with the subject of Ruby Gale. It's all I've heard for the last several hours."

"You don't like playing second fiddle, is that it?" he mocked.

"Think what you like." She refused to argue about it. "You may find her to be a scintillating topic of conversation, but I don't. Good night."

"Good night," he returned. Before she had taken a step past him, he asked, "Is Pet a nickname?"

She was surprised by the personal question, or perhaps by the genuine interest in his voice. "In a way, it is. It's a shortened version of Petra, my given name." She tipped her head curiously to one side and frowned. "Why?"

"No special reason. I just wondered," he shrugged. "There's a meeting at seven o'clock in the morning."

"Yes, I know," Pet nodded, and glanced over her shoulder toward the restaurant. "Were you just going in for dinner?"

"No. As a matter of fact, I was just on my way out of the hotel." The glint in his eye seemed a little bit wicked, although his expression was impassively bland. "I'm dining with Miss Gale this evening."

His announcement seemed almost the last straw. First the crew, many of whom she had numbered as her friends, had talked of nothing but Ruby Gale. Now Dane Kingston was having dinner with her. The defection of a man Pet really didn't like was the hardest to take.

Her gaze swept over him, noting that he hadn't changed out of the brushed denims and plaid shirt. "You're going in that?" she questioned icily.

"It's informal." A smile tugged at the corners of his mouth without really showing itself. "We're just having some sandwiches in her suite."

"What? No champagne and caviar?" There was a certain acidity to her murmured taunt.

"That's being saved to celebrate the completion of the special," Dane responded easily.

"How nice. Enjoy your evening," she said, and hurried on her way before he could stop her again.

It was too early to go to bed. After twenty minutes in the small hotel room the walls began to close in on her. Jamming her writing pad and paperback book in her large shoulder bag, Pet left the room and went out of the hotel through a side door leading to the pool area.

There were two families with children swimming in the pool, but few of the deck chairs were occupied. Pet chose one with a small wrought-iron table beside it. It was nearly a full hour before sundown on this warm summer evening — not that it mattered, since the pool area was lighted.

Shedding her blazer, Pet settled into the deck chair and got out her writing pad. She had barely written "Dear Rudy" when a shadow was cast across the paper. She looked up to find Joe Wiles's wide bulk standing beside her chair.

"Writing love letters?" he smiled.

"It's to my brother. He's in the coast guard. Right now he's stationed in Texas, along the Gulf Coast," she explained. "Are you taking an evening stroll?"

"Yeah, I'm taking my nightly constitutional before turning in," he grinned, and pulled up a chair to sit beside her. "Do you have any other brothers or sisters?"

"An older brother, Hugh. He lives in Connecticut, married with three kids — all boys. His wife, Marjorie, is a fantastic girl. We all love her. Do you want to see some pictures of my nephews?" she asked.

At his nod, she reached in her bag and took out the small photo album to show him the trio of boys with the Wallis blond hair and green eyes. Then Joe took his billfold out of his hip pocket and showed her pictures of his grandchildren, all seven of them.

"How come you aren't married, Pet? You

should have pictures of your own kids to show off, instead of your brother's. I hope you aren't one of those modern females who don't want to get married," Joe stated with a disapproving frown.

"You sound like my dad! I hear this lecture every weekend about the blissful state of matrimony." There was a laughing twinkle in her eyes. "I can't seem to convince him or mom that I'd get married in a minute if the right man asked."

"Somebody must have asked you before now," he insisted. "You're a lovely creature."

"Thanks. I have been asked," Pet admitted. "I was even engaged for a year, but it didn't work out."

"It must have been very painful."

"Strangely, it wasn't," she remembered. "I really liked Bob. As a matter of fact we're still very good friends. When we mutually decided to call off the engagement, I was sorry — disappointed that it hadn't worked for us — but my heart wasn't broken. It wasn't even cracked or bruised. Which proves it would have been a mistake to marry him."

"I guess so," he agreed with regret.

"I think I'll have a Coke. Would you like one, Joe?" she offered, and reached in her purse to get change for the drink machine standing against the exterior wall of the hotel.

"No, thanks," he refused, and pressed a hand against his rotund stomach. "Those carbonated beverages give me heartburn."

There was a definite golden cast to the western sky. Pet noticed it when she walked back to her chair after getting the cold can of soda. For a fleeting second she allowed herself to wonder whether Dane and Ruby were admiring the sunset together in her suite.

"Why do you suppose Dane Kingston has never married, Joe?" she asked with absent curiosity. "Or has he been?"

"Not that I know about," he answered her last question first. "Could be his reason is the same as yours — never met the right girl. He's certainly had more than his share of beautiful women hanging on his arm over the years."

"And probably hopping into his bed, too," Pet added on a note of disgust. "I'll bet no one has ever said yes to him, because he's too bossy and pushy. A woman can't tolerate that for long."

Joe shook his head in disagreement. "In this life you have to go after what you want. Nobody is going to hand it to you. I admire the way Dane never lets anything stand in the way of what he wants. He knows what it is and goes for it. I like that. There are very few men like him in this world."

"That's heartening," Pet murmured dryly.

"I'm not going to argue with you about him," Joe declared, and pushed to his feet. "I'd better finish my stroll and let you finish that letter to your brother. Good night, Pet."

"Good night." But it was several minutes before she reached for her pen and resumed the letter to Rudy.

Chapter Four

The orchestra was positioned to the rear of the stage, the pianist testing a few quick chords to loosen his tension. The dancers in their practice leotards were posed around Ruby Gale, standing at front center stage. Beyond them the backup vocal group was fanned out.

This was a practice session, a dry run before tomorrow's dress rehearsal and the following night's concert. Each one of the songs and dance routines would be performed so camera angles could be corrected and the lighting adjusted.

The cameras were warmed up. Everyone on stage was waiting for the cue from Claude, the floor director. Dane Kingston was in the control booth in the van parked outside. It was his instructions and directions that were coming over Pet's headset.

"Camera two, we'll be opening with you," he informed Pet. "I want a close-up shot of Miss Gale, widening on my order. We'll be coming to you next, camera three. All right, we've been through this number twice already. I want the tape rolling on this one."

Pet nibbled at her lower lip, tension building as she rechecked her focus. She knew the procedure. The practice tape would be made and reviewed later that night for any final changes in angle or lighting. All of tomorrow's dress rehearsal would be taped, since the concert show was a one-time performance. There were a dozen things that could ruin a song at a live show. In that event, the dress-rehearsal tapes would be a backup that could be edited into the final product.

"Tape is rolling," Dane stated.

"Let's have it quiet!" Claude instructed the cast, and absolute silence descended on the center.

From this point on, the only voice would be Dane's as he communicated with the cameras, Claude, the sound man and the lights. Mentally Pet blocked out everything else. Someone else would be responsible for the quality of the sound, the tempo of the music and the volume of the singer on stage.

"All right, two." Dane's voice was calm, and Pet relaxed, too, now that the taping had begun. She didn't notice the signal Claude gave, nor hear the heavy beat of the base drum begin the song. The titian-haired Ruby Gale filled her camera lens, inviting and beguiling blue eyes staring straight at the camera.

As she began to sing the first lyric, Dane ordered, "Widen the shot, two! *Slowly*," he emphasized, then a little sternly as she began to reverse the zoom, "Don't lose focus, Wallis! Camera three, get ready. We're coming to you. *Now!*"

Pet didn't need to consult the paper clipped to her camera, listing the various angles of her coverage in this song. The next one was to be an overall shot of the entire stage, including the orchestra and performers, then narrowing in to isolate the star singing within the circle of male dancers.

"Hold the shot, two. We're on you," Dane advised. "When she moves stage left, go with her, Wallis." Pet tried, not very successfully, as Dane's angry voice informed her, "You're letting her get behind a dancer. Three, take it on the turn — quick! You blew that shot, Wallis."

She gritted her teeth, not convinced the fault had been entirely hers. She suspected the dancer had been out of position, although no one was ever precisely where he was supposed to be. Either way, there wasn't time to dwell on who had been in error. She had to be in position for her next shot.

Meanwhile, she listened to Dane heaping praise on Andy. "Great shot, one." The even pitch of his voice didn't change, although a level of amusement entered it. "I didn't know you had it in you, Turner. You'd better make certain you can do that again." Then, crisply, "You're off center, Wallis. I can't come to you until you have Ruby in the middle. You've got it!"

Concentrating, Pet followed the star through her next sequence of steps and its accompanying song lyrics. Her coverage was flawless.

But she didn't receive the deserved praise from the control booth; Dane's attention was occupied elsewhere.

"Baxter, you're in three's picture. Duck behind the reed section," he ordered the cameraman on stage with the handheld camera. "Okay, three, it's yours."

As the song drew to an end, Pet's was the last shot. It was to be a close-up on the star while she belted out the last line, then opening to full length and finally widening to full stage. The first Pet executed perfectly but she faltered on the second.

On the third, Dane was barking in her ear, "Loosen it up, two! I said, loosen it up," he complained. "Hold it!" The song was finished. There was a mental countdown ticking in everyone's head. Then Dane gave the order, "Stop tape."

"Good job!" Claude called to the performers on stage.

His voice unfroze them from their positions. There was an instant gabble of voices and movement everywhere. Pet released an unconscious sigh and turned off her camera. The tension of needing to be as soundless as possible had been lifted.

A public-address system had been connected between the stage and the control van to extend Dane's communication link to the performers. It was switched on now and his voice filled the theater.

"That was a great number. You were sensational, Ruby," he praised her.

The compliment brought a radiant smile to the star. She blew a kiss in the direction of the loudspeaker over which his voice had been projected, and glided into the wings. Just as quickly, the PA system was switched off and Dane's voice was again restricted to the headsets of the crew.

"Claude, get the group set up for the next number," he advised the floor director.

But it was Lon Baxter's voice that dominated the earphones. "Hot damn! Did you guys watch her strutting through that number? She sent my blood pressure soaring!" His compliments became punctuated with swearwords, as if vulgarity somehow emphasized his enthusiasm.

"Let's clean up the language!" Dane snapped. "You're forgetting, Baxter, that there's a lady listening."

"A lady?" Lon questioned, then hooted, "You mean Pet?"

"That's exactly who I mean!" was Dane's angry and silencing retort.

In the past, Pet had always turned a deaf ear to that kind of language rather than inhibit her male coworkers. If they weren't able to talk freely, she had always felt she would be driving a wedge between herself and them. So she didn't welcome this interference from Dane Kingston.

"Don't worry about it, fellas," she said into her microphone. "I have special earphones that automatically censor any words that might shock my virgin ears. All I hear is a confusing set of bleeps."

"Miss Wallis —" Dane's voice came low and threatening over the headset "— I give the orders around here. It's of little interest to me whether you would be offended or not. As long as I'm running this show, there isn't going to be any more of that kind of language around a woman. Is that clear?"

"Perfectly." She ground the response through her teeth, crimsoning at his sharp reproof.

"Now that we all understand one another, let's get ready for the next number. Ruby is doing a solo on stage. You shouldn't have any trouble this time, Wallis, in making sure no one else blocks the star out of your shot," he suggested sarcastically.

Pet seethed at that totally unjustified slur on her ability, and clamped her teeth down hard to hold back a sassing reply. She had already been the recipient of several rebukes from him and she didn't intend to invite another.

But it seemed nothing went right after that. One major production number went continuously wrong. Either a dancer missed a cue, or Ruby Gale muffed the lyrics, or the assigned camera lost the shot — usually Pet, it seemed. Finally Claude murmured to Dane that maybe it was time for a midafternoon break since their star was showing signs of screaming.

The minute Dane voiced a reluctant agreement, Pet tugged her headset off and hopped down from the platform. Her long blond ponytail was swinging back and forth like a cat's tail lashing in anger as she walked swiftly down the aisle for a tall cup of iced tea.

Without saying a word or waiting to see if anyone wanted to join her, she pushed out of an exit door and walked outside. Frustrated by her own apparent inability to do her job right and angered by the way Dane kept pointing it out to her, she needed to escape the tense and stifling atmosphere inside the building.

It was a hot July afternoon, but the air was fresh, circulated by a gentle breeze. She found a shady place to sit where the breeze reached her, and lighted a cigarette, hoping the nicotine would calm her jangled nerves. Some of the others wandered outside, as well. When Charlie walked over to enjoy the shade she had found, Lon and two others followed him.

"It may be hotter out here, but it's a lot more peaceful," Charlie sighed.

"It's a good thing Claude suggested a fifteen-minute break," Lon remarked. "We came very close to seeing that temper Andy has been telling us our star has. You should have heard some of the things she said to that poor dancer who forgot the routine! If Dane thought my language was out of line, he should have heard some of the words Ruby Gale used."

Pet wished he hadn't brought that earlier matter up. As if he realized what he had said, Lon glanced at her, noting her strained and downcast expression. A rueful grimace twisted his mouth.

"I guess I do owe you an apology, Pet. Some of the things I said were really off color. I forget sometimes that you're not one of the boys. I'm sorry," he offered.

"Forget it. I have." She crushed out the tasteless cigarette.

"I agree with you, Lon," Charlie inserted. "Dane was right to remind us that Pet's a woman. A lot of times we don't show her the respect that we should."

"Listen, I've never asked for any special treatment from you guys," she reminded them.

"If you think I'm going to open a door for you, you're crazy," Lon joked, trying to make Pet see the situation with a little humor.

"Sorry, I'm a little touchy. It's been a rotten day what with Kingston constantly harping on me," Pet explained with a genuine effort to contain her irritation. "I can't seem to do anything right."

"Maybe you're trying too hard," Charlie suggested.

"It sure sounded like Dane was singling Pet out for more than her share of criticism. Of course, that's just my opinion," Lon shrugged. "I don't know how it looked on the monitors. Maybe you had it coming."

"I just wish he'd quit picking on me — in general," Pet sighed. "I can take criticism, but I'd like a pat on the head every now and then."

"Don't let him get to you," Charlie urged, and rubbed a comforting hand on her shoulder. "You're good at what you do. Just remember that."

"Hey!" Claude stuck his head out of the exit door. "Everybody back inside. Let's get to work!"

Pet followed the crew inside and took one last drink of her iced tea before throwing the cup in the wastebasket. Then it was back on the platform to warm the camera up and try the same number that proverbial "one more time."

The short break didn't seem to improve anything. By the end of the day she was a ball of nerves, stretched thin and coiled tight. As always, the ride back to the hotel was noisy, which didn't help. The crew tended to make up for so many hours of enforced silence by laughing and joking at a fever pitch of excitement. Usually such gaiety was the ideal means of relieving their stress, but it didn't work for Pet this time.

At the hotel she didn't dawdle in the lobby or corridor with the boys, but went straight to her room and almost directly into the shower. She didn't take the time to dry her long hair. Instead she wound it into a golden brown bun on top of her head, crisscrossing a pair of jade pokes through it for an Oriental look. Her jade silk blouse buttoned up the front with a mandarin collar and a hand-embroidered water lily on the left side. The top was complemented by a pair of mother-of-pearl slacks. It was usually a morale-boosting outfit that enhanced her proud carriage, but she didn't feel any better when she studied her reflection in the mirror.

Sighing, Pet left her hotel room. Too on edge to have dinner yet, she decided to stop in the lounge and have a relaxing before-dinner cocktail with the boys. Her plans went awry when she walked into the dimly lighted bar and didn't see Charlie, Andy or any of the regular group. At a table near the bar she noticed Claude, Joe Wiles, Dane Kingston and the audio man, Greg Coopster, all seated together.

She started to leave, then decided to have a quiet drink by herself; after all, that was the reason she had come into the lounge. When Joe spoke and the others glanced around, Pet just nodded. She didn't approach their table as she made her way to a secluded booth in the corner. The barmaid came to take her order.

"A glass of sherry, please." Why on earth had she ordered that, Pet wondered when the miniskirted girl had walked away. Was she trying to prove what a 'proper' lady she was?

Reaching for the pack of cigarettes in her purse, she shook one out. The lighter flamed with a quick snap. As she lifted the light to the cigarette, a shadow blocked what little light reached the corner booth. Her hand began to shake even before she looked to see who was there.

Because she had already guessed it was Dane Kingston. Lowering the hand holding the cigarette to the table to hide its trembling, she slowly turned her head to meet his gaze. The forbidding thinness of his mouth didn't make her feel any more comfortable. He bent forward to lean a hand on the table. It was an action that struck her as threatening despite his cold attempt at a smile.

"Would you care to join us, Miss Wallis?" he invited.

"No." She didn't temper the flat refusal and looked away to take another puff from her cigarette, pretending to ignore him. Which was an impossibility.

"I insist," Dane commanded firmly. "You shouldn't sit alone in a strange bar."

"You're impossible, do you know that?" Pet flared, unleashing the anger she had kept bottled up inside her all day. "First you criticize me for being the sole female drinking with a group of men I happen to work with, saying that it didn't look ladylike. Now you're upset because I'm here alone. Why don't you make up your mind?"

She didn't like the sudden flash of amusement that glittered in his dark eyes. Agitated, she looked away again. "Nothing I do ever pleases you," she complained bitterly.

The barmaid came back with her glass of sherry. Dane had to move to one side so she could serve it. After the girl had left, instead of resuming his former position, he slid onto the booth seat beside Pet. Initially she was too startled to offer a protest. Once she felt the contact of his hard thigh alongside hers, she couldn't seem to breathe, let alone speak.

Aware that his head was turned so he could watch her, Pet stared at the glass of sherry sitting on the cocktail napkin. She didn't even notice the ashes building up on the end of her cigarette or the gray blue smoke curling from its tip. His gaze was making a slow inspection of her profile; she could feel it as certainly as if he were touching her.

"Do you want to please me?" The drawled question suggested intimacy lightly spiced with a vague curiosity.

His implication sent her imagination off on a forbidden tangent. If he could affect her this deeply just by sitting next to her and hinting at familiarity, how would she feel if he made love to her? Her heart knocked against her ribs.

"I couldn't care less," she lied, impatient with herself for being physically disturbed by him. It gave false credence to her statement. She reached for the sherry glass. "Why don't you go away and leave me alone? I was doing fine before you came along."

"A woman alone in a bar is a target for any man who walks in. You can't sit here by yourself," Dane insisted, gently this time.

But it only increased his attraction and made her all the more determined to resist it. "Did it ever occur to you that maybe I wanted to be picked up by some — traveling salesman?" she challenged angrily.

His gaze narrowed to bore relentlessly all the way to her soul. "Is that what you want?"

Bravado failed her, but she managed to hold on to her poise. "All I wanted was a quiet drink before dinner and a chance to relax. If you're finally satisfied, will you please leave?"

"I'm not going to let you sit here by yourself. Bring your sherry over to my table. We're going over tomorrow's schedule," Dane told her.

Sighing, Pet could see that she had about as much chance of persuading him to leave as she did of moving a mountain. If she couldn't move the mountain, the only alternative was to remove herself.

"You obviously didn't hear me. I said I wanted a quiet drink and a chance to relax. Neither would be possible in the middle of a technical discussion," she retorted, and opened her purse to take out the money for her drink and leave it on the table. "Would you please get out of my way so I can leave?"

"But you haven't had your drink." His gaze roamed over her face, stubbornly not moving until he found out her intentions.

"I'm taking it into the restaurant with me. Surely it can't be a crime if a woman has a glass of sherry in the restaurant before dining alone?" Pet challenged.

"It might be a shame, but I don't think it's a crime," he agreed, the corners of his mouth twitching slightly in amusement.

"Then would you mind getting up so I can leave?" she demanded in a voice that was growing steadily thinner with the strain of his nearness.

With the suggestion of a smile still playing at his mouth, Dane slid his brawny frame out of the booth and rolled effortlessly to his feet. The touch of his hand was pleasantly firm as he helped her out.

"We'll be playing today's tapes about an hour from now in one of the meeting rooms to make any last-minute changes. If you're through with dinner by then, you can join us." He didn't release his hold of her elbow even though she was standing and didn't require his assistance anymore.

His fingers transmitted the natural warmth generated by his body and sent it spreading up her arm. It made her flesh tingle quite pleasurably. Briefly, she was tempted by the prospect of spending more time in his company until she remembered the tapes they would be viewing. She had endured enough of his criticism for one day.

"Is that an order?" she questioned, turning to pick up her drink and thus forcing him to release her arm.

"No, you aren't required to attend." Something flickered in his look — displeasure, perhaps.

"Then I respectfully decline," Pet replied with faint mockery. "Excuse me."

Pausing long enough to inform the barmaid that she was taking her drink into the restaurant, she entered the dining room through the connecting door to the lounge. She did eat alone. It wasn't until the waiter brought her coffee that any of the crew arrived. Pet could have joined them, but there wasn't any point.

Too restless to return to her room, she wasn't in the mood for the kind of shoptalk the group would be having in the lounge, so she wandered outside to stroll around the pool area and watch the sunset from a lounge chair. Reentering the hotel, she stopped by the small gift shop and newsstand to look around.

Ruby Gale's face stared at her from the cover of a movie magazine. Curious, Pet leafed through the pages to find the article about the star. Several photographs of Ruby accompanied the write-up. One of them was a picture of the redhead and Dane Kingston lying side by side on a beach mat. Ruby Gale was wearing the scantiest bikini Pet had ever seen, but it wasn't the woman that riveted her attention.

It was Dane in his dark swimming trunks. Lean and powerful muscles rippled across his chest and shoulders and held his stomach flat. The implied strength in the sinewed columns of his legs reminded Pet of nude sculptures she had seen of Greek gods. The tight-fitting material of his swimming trunks molded his narrow hips, sending her blood pounding with its emphasis of his virile, male shape.

She quickly studied his expression. He wasn't smiling, but there was a self-satisfied look about him that indicated just as plainly that he was enjoying himself. And the lazy way his eyes were lingering on the woman beside him indicated that she was the cause of his pleasure.

Irritated at herself for becoming so absorbed in the photograph of him, Pet abruptly closed the magazine and set it back on the shelf. She was adult, no longer given to crushes on men who were unattainable. But was he unattainable, a little voice argued. She ignored the question. That kind of thinking would ultimately bring her grief. Before leaving, she bought a pack of cigarettes and promised herself she'd stop smoking soon.

Crossing the lobby, she turned down the main corridor of the hotel. Joe Wiles walked out of a meeting room, leaving the door ajar, and started down the hall ahead of her. Pet glanced in the room as she went by, but there was only a member of the hotel staff inside, emptying ashtrays and carrying away the coffee cups. She quickened her steps to catch up with the heavyset man.

"How did the meeting go?" she asked.

The carpeted hallway had muffled her footsteps. Joe's balding head turned with a jerk at her question.

"You startled me," he accused without anger.

"Sorry. Did you make many changes after you saw the tapes?" She walked with him. For the time being, they were both going in the same direction.

"Surprisingly, very few, and most of those were minor," he replied. "Audio has some problems that they have to correct, but Dane was satisfied with the video. He's going to experiment with the switcher tomorrow, try for some different effects on the solo numbers."

"But it looked good?" Pet persisted. It didn't seem possible that Dane was as satisfied with the results as Joe implied.

"Of course. Did you think it wouldn't?" His smile was a little confused. "It will be even better tomorrow. Having everyone in costume will really make a difference in the finished product."

"Yes, I know it will," she agreed absently.

"What time does the dining room close?" Joe glanced at his watch. "I haven't eaten yet and I'm starved."

"I think they stop serving at eleven."

"I'd better hurry." He raised an eyebrow. "I'd like at least to wash and change my shirt before I eat."

They reached the point where the corridor branched into two separate halls. Pet turned left. "I'll see you in the morning, Joe."

"Good night." He waved.

Arriving at the door to her room, she searched through the bottom of her bag for the key. Just as she found it, the door opened in the room directly opposite the hall from hers, and Dane stepped out.

"Is that your room?" Pet blurted in surprise.

"Yes, conveniently located to keep an eye on you." The corners of his eyes crinkled with a smile.

She hadn't expected him to admit such a thing. His frankness irritated her. She turned to unlock her door.

"As you can see, I'm retiring for the night — all alone — without any of the boys tagging after me. You don't have to worry about checking on me tonight."

"I'm not checking on you," Dane chuckled. "It's purely coincidence that my room is across the hall."

Instead of feeling better, she felt worse. She had been foolish to believe he was so concerned about her that he was virtually standing guard over her. To add to her difficulties, the lock was being its usual stubborn self and resisting her attempts to turn the key. Dane was watching her struggle with it, which made Pet even more uncomfortable.

She tried to urge him on his way. "If you're going to the dining room to eat, you'd better hurry. I think they stop serving at eleven."

"I'm not on my way to the restaurant." He

crossed the hall. "Give me the key. There's a trick to unlocking hotel doors."

It was simpler to hand him the key than to argue, so she did. "Have you had dinner already?" she frowned. "I thought the meeting finished only a little while ago. I just met Joe in the hall."

"It just broke up," he agreed, and inserted the key in the lock again. "And no, I haven't had dinner."

She studied his bent head and the curling thickness of his dark brown hair, and her hands itched to run their fingers through his hair and feel those vigorous strands beneath her palms. She was shaken by the force of that unbidden desire. She clenched her hands tightly around her bag in case she unconsciously gave in to it.

"You have to eat." She tried to concentrate on the subject. "It isn't healthy to skip meals."

With a deft twist of his wrist he turned the key in the lock and pushed her door open. "Don't worry. I'll have room service send a sandwich or something up to the suite," he promised smoothly as he turned to face her.

"The suite?" she repeated. Separated from him by only a few feet, she noticed the shadows along his cheeks. The lights overhead were bright, clearly illuminating his rugged features. The darkness was obviously caused by a fast-growing beard.

Her thoughts returned to the implication of

his statement. "Then you're on your way to Miss Gale's hotel."

"Yes," he nodded, and moved out of her doorway. "At this hour?" She said exactly what was on her mind and instantly regretted it. "I'm sorry, it's really none of my business."

"It isn't," Dane agreed, but he regarded her with lazy indulgence rather than anger. "After viewing the tapes tonight, I have a couple of things I want to suggest to her before tomorrow's dress rehearsal and taping."

"You don't have to explain to me." Pet didn't want him lying and making up excuses. Surely he realized that she had heard the gossip about the torrid affair he was having with Ruby Gale!

She had taken one step across the threshold into her room when his finger touched her chin and turned her head to look at him.

"Don't I?" he queried softly.

He was suddenly very close. His rough male features seemed to fill her vision, leaving room for nothing else. Alarm fluttered her pulse, sending danger signals through her veins. She didn't dare believe what her senses were saying. Dane was on his way to see Ruby Gale. She mustn't forget that, or that photograph of the two of them in the magazine.

"Don't you think you should shave first?" she suggested with an admirable degree of calm.

His hand was removed from her chin to rub his cheek. The action produced a faint rasping sound of beard stubble scraping across his skin.

84

He seemed to have been unaware of the growth until she called his attention to it.

"Does it bother you if a man shows up to see you with a five o'clock shadow?" he asked.

"It doesn't bother me," she shrugged. "But I'm not Miss Gale."

"No, you aren't." When he took a step forward, Pet took one backwards and bumped against the door. "Your key."

She felt foolish for retreating like a timid schoolgirl before her first kiss when she saw the room key in his hand. Her fingers loosened their death grip on her handbag to reach for it but they weren't given the chance to take it from him, because the key was forgotten entirely as he lowered his mouth onto hers, blotting out everything.

A splintering shock held her motionless until the warm taste of his mouth melted her stiffness. She responded easily to the persuasive ardor of his kiss, a glow spreading through her veins. There was even pleasure in the light scrape of his beard against her soft skin. Desire grew within her to deepen the kiss, to realize the potential delirium that it promised.

Something cold and flat slipped inside her blouse where the top set of buttons was unfastened. Her skin shrank from the contact, but couldn't elude it. It took her a dazed second to identify the object as a metal key. The discovery was followed close on the heels by the realization that Dane's fingers were guiding it inside the left undercup of her bra.

Before she could protest his flagrantly intimate action, Dane was lifting his head and withdrawing his hand from inside her blouse. She tried to look indignant, but she wasn't very successful — the smoldering gleam in his dark eyes told her so.

As if to prove how completely within his spell she was, he circled her left breast with his large hand. The possession was light, in no way forcing her to endure his caress, while claiming his right to do so.

"Now you've finally pleased me, Pet," he murmured in a voice that nearly melted her knees. "Get a good night's sleep, hmm?"

While she was still trying to surface, he was moving away from her and striding down the hall. In a wonderful kind of daze she stepped the rest of the way into her room and closed the door, trying to figure out how it had all happened and what it meant.

The first was easy because she recalled vividly the comment she had made in the bar that she couldn't please him. She remembered that Dane had asked if she wanted to. If that kiss was a sample, she definitely wanted to please him.

But why had he kissed her? Because she was an attractive woman and willing to be kissed? There was nothing wrong with that: it was a normal, healthy reaction. Except that Pet hoped it was more than that. She didn't like to consider the possibility that it might never happen again.

Sighing, she turned to bolt and latch the door. The action caused the room key to jab its point into the soft curve of her breast. She reached inside her blouse to take it out and return it to its rightful place in her handbag.

Chapter Five

The next morning it was work as usual, with a meeting scheduled first thing to go over the few changes. Other than a vague smile and nod in her direction, Dane paid no more attention to Pet than to any other member of the crew. She tried to tell herself that she wasn't disappointed, that she hadn't really expected anything different.

In an effort to show she was heart-whole and carefree, Pet threw herself into her job and worked to establish the old camaraderie with the boys. She had kissed men before without it meaning anything and forgotten it the next day. She could do so again.

It was later in the morning before they were ready to actually begin taping the dress rehearsal. The production crew had plenty to do to keep busy while the cast spent their time in Makeup and Wardrobe.

All the performers were finally on stage for the opening number except for the star, Ruby Gale. When she walked out to take her position, Pet gave an audible gasp at the gown the redhead was wearing. At first glance it didn't appear to have any sides. She stared to see why it didn't flap open and that was when she noticed the flesh-colored netting at the sides.

An assortment of reactions came over her headset from the male members of the production crew. They ranged from a breathless "Wow!" to "Sweet momma!" Amusement deepened the corners of her mouth and sent a sparkle of laughter into her green eyes.

"If I didn't know better, gang," Pet murmured teasingly into the small microphone, "I'd swear I was receiving an obscene phone call, with all this heavy breathing that's going on!"

"What's keeping that dress on?" Lon groaned.

"It must be glued." Charlie made a choked guess.

"It's sheer willpower, fellas," Pet teased, not explaining that the three-inch-wide strip of skin they saw on either side was not bare flesh but covered with netting.

Dane's voice briskly inserted itself. "Cut the chatter," he ordered. "Get the white boards up. I want color checks on these cameras again. Joe, I'm getting a hot spot on the vocal group. What's wrong?"

His briskness snapped them into action. But it didn't end the speculation or the avid interest in the daring gown and the stunning creature wearing it. Absent comments continued to find their way into the otherwise technical communication over the headset.

"If it's glued on, what do you suppose is going to happen if she starts perspiring?"

Charlie wondered. "Do you think it will stay on? Will the glue hold?"

"Oh, Joe, turn up the lights and bake this stage," Lon pleaded. "Turn this into a sweat bath."

"Then bring in the fans," Andy inserted.

"All this panting is going to melt my earphones, guys," Pet warned on an impish note.

"I said cut the chatter, Wallis!" Dane barked in her ear.

It didn't matter that he was out in the large van where she couldn't see him. A mental image of him sprang into her mind — his mouth hard and tight-lipped and his dark eyes blazing. Pet was stung by the injustice of being singled out by his barbed tongue.

"Why pick on me?" she griped to herself, but forgot to push the highly sensitive microphone away from her lips. "I'm just about the only one whose eyes haven't popped out of his head."

Since she hadn't intended her comment to be heard by anyone, she visibly jerked when Dane answered her question. "That is exactly the reason. The others can't help themselves, but you can, Wallis. So straighten up!"

"Yes, sir! Anything you say, *sir!*" She masked her angry defiance with exaggerated obedience that left no one in doubt of her temper.

Any question about what last night's kiss might have meant no longer existed. As far as Pet was concerned, the meaning was clear: it had been nothing more than a passing whim. Dane was going to be hard and rough on her today to make sure she understood that and didn't get any ideas. The message was loud and clear. Pet was neither deaf nor stupid. After all, she hadn't really thought she could successfully compete with that red-haired sex goddess on stage. And she hadn't forgotten that Dane had been with Ruby Gale after he had left her.

It was another ten minutes before the floor director told the performers to take their positions on stage for the opening number. When Dane informed the crew that the tape was rolling, Claude asked for quiet and began the countdown: "Ten, nine, eight, seven, six. . . ." He stopped there and continued it with his fingers, so his voice wouldn't be picked up on tape.

All that was mainly for the performers' benefit. Dane was issuing his own instructions prior to that. "Do you remember the sequence of the opening number, Wallis? A close-up frame of Ruby. Open it *when* I tell you and the *way* I tell you or I'll strangle you with my bare hands," he warned, and began counting. "Ten, nine, eight. . . ." It was his countdown that the floor director repeated.

So it began. If Pet thought he had been demanding the day before, it was mild compared to the relentless way he drove the crew today. The slightest flaw or imperfection in a shot drew sharp and immediate criticism. Although everyone felt the razor edge of his tongue at some point, the majority of his censure seemed to go to Pet.

Take after take, number after number, Dane pushed them. Even when the fault belonged to the star, Ruby Gale, for missing her spot on stage or going beyond it out of camera range, it was the crew he blamed over the loudspeaker system. A couple of times Ruby flubbed the song lyrics.

Over the PA speaker Dane's voice was benevolent and forgiving as it filled the theater. "Don't worry about it, Ruby. After all the mistakes we've made, you're entitled to blow one now and then. You're perfect. You're doing great."

Silently Pet seethed at this preferential treatment for the star. Nothing remotely resembling a critical word was ever directed at Ruby Gale. Why couldn't Dane snap at her the way he did everyone else, she thought angrily. In his eyes Ruby Gale could do no wrong, while Pet couldn't seem to do anything right. She felt raw, suffering from a thousand needling remarks, oversensitized by a barrage of pinpricks.

She had the closing shot on another production number. "Hold that frame, camera two," Dane's voice advised sternly in her ear. "Hold it. Hold it!" Impatience inched into his tone and scraped at her nerves. "Okay, stop tape."

At the statement, Pet immediately closed her eyes and lowered her chin in wary relief. Her long blond ponytail swung forward to brush the top of her left shoulder. Releasing her grip on the control handles of the camera, she wiped her sweaty palms on the legs of her faded denims. She straightened to glance across the rows of seats to Andy's camera position and he gave her a crooked smile and a thumbs-up signal.

"We made it through that one," his voice murmured through her earphones.

Before she could reply, Dane's voice came over the public-address system. "Good job, gang. I think we've earned a twenty-minute break."

The richly resonant pitch of his voice vibrated over Pet. "Ah, a voice from above," Charlie joked, and lifted his hands in mock awe.

"Regardless of what he thinks, he isn't related to God Almighty," Pet muttered, assuming that Dane had already removed his headset after announcing the break.

Her mistake was quickly pointed out to her by Dane himself. "If I was related to him, Wallis, I would use my influence with him to do something about you," he said curtly. "And the next time I tell you to hold a shot, that doesn't mean you should move."

She wanted to scream at him to stop criticizing everything she did and to tell him that she had read between the lines and knew he wasn't romantically interested in her. Some perverse streak made her do just the opposite.

"Darling, it isn't any good," she cooed over the headset mike. "Everyone has guessed that you're madly in love with me. Trying to hide it by yelling at me all the time isn't fooling anybody. We can't keep it a secret anymore."

There was an incredulous laugh from someone, but it wasn't Dane. Pet knew she had invited his wrath upon her and grimly tugged off her headset. With her mouth clamped tightly shut, she hopped off the platform into the aisle.

Charlie called to her, still wearing his headset. "Hey, Pet! Dane wants to talk to you!"

Holding her head at a proudly defiant angle, she didn't slow her strides as she yelled back, "Tell him that's tough! I'm on my break!"

At the refreshment table set up for the crew, Pet skipped the insulated container of iced tea in favor of the coffee urn. It was left over from the morning break, which made it strong and inky black. Pet felt in need of its strength.

"What got into you, Pet?" Charlie came up to stand beside her. The smile on his face seemed to be there in spite of his better judgment. It was as if he admired her for talking back while he thought she was crazy for doing so.

Lon was there, shaking his head. "You really believe in flying in the face of danger, don't you?"

"I just want him off my back," she grumbled, and swore under her breath when she tried to take a drink of the scalding black coffee and burned her tongue.

The explosion of a door being forcefully slammed shut thundered through the cavernous theater and echoed in shock waves. A quick glance over her shoulder saw Dane striding toward them. Squaring around, Pet kept her back to him and hooked a thumb through the belt loop of her jeans, trying to adopt an attitude of nonchalance while studying the black liquid in her cup.

"I'm afraid you're in for it, Pet," Andy murmured, glancing at her over the rim of his drink.

With an exaggerated blink of her eyes, she pretended she didn't care. The skin along the back of her neck prickled a warning. Out of her side vision she saw Dane stop on her right, but she wouldn't look at him.

"You didn't really think you were going to get by with that, did you?" Dane sounded remarkably calm as he made the low challenge.

There wasn't an adequate reply she could make to that, so she didn't try. To cover her silence, she started to raise the cup of coffee to her mouth, but Dane reached out to take it from her.

"Hey! That's my coffee." When she tried to hold onto it, the hot coffee sloshed over the side and burned her hand, forcing her to let go. "Ouch!"

"Hold this." Dane handed the cup to Andy,

then turned back to her. She was wary of the glint in his eye and the hint of a smile on his mouth. "How wonderful that everyone knows and I don't have to hide it," he taunted softly.

In the next second his hand had clamped itself on her arm to pull her toward him. Her protesting outcry was choked off by shock at the form his retaliation was taking. She tried to ward off his chest with her hands, but she was no match for his sheer brute force. His palm cupped the back of her head to hold it still, his fingers tangling in the length of her hair, while his mouth made an unerring descent onto hers.

The encircling steel band of his arm held her fast, arching her waist to bring her more fully against him. Pet had expected his kiss to be a bruising and punishing assault. There was driving force, but no brutality. He dominated her lips, moving over them as if satisfying a burning need to consume their softness. Her senses were filled with the sensation of his hard length bent protectively over hers, the thrust of his hips, and the solid muscles of his torso flattening her small breasts.

Aware of the interested spectators watching the embrace, Pet pushed at him, but the only surface available to her hands was the sides of his waist. It was an ineffectual attempt that gained nothing at all. Not that she really minded; the things his kiss was doing to her rivaled her imagination. The wild singing in her veins was hotly sweet, searing her with a buoyancy that convinced her she was floating on a cloud. She stopped resisting and began kissing him back, her hunger matching his appetite.

Before her hands could begin their final, submissive curve around his middle, Dane was drawing away. There was a disturbed roughness to his breathing and the smoldering darkness of passion in his eyes. Yet the clearest impression Pet had was the scattered cheers and applause of those around them.

The crew regarded the kiss as a huge joke, thinking that Dane had deftly turned the tables on her. And it was true. The heat of embarrassment rushed into her face, staining her cheeks scarlet. Pet couldn't remember ever blushing in her life, but she had never made such a fool of herself. For a few seconds she had forgotten all that had gone before the kiss.

She lowered her gaze to the tanned hollow of his throat, his arms still containing her within their circle.

"Why did you do that?" she asked huskily. Had she really deserved this kind of humiliation?

Dane crooked a finger under her chin and forced her to look at him before he would answer her question. "It seemed the most effective way of shutting up a smart mouth." The lazy glint in his dark eyes seemed to hold only amusement at her discomfort. "And if you do it again, the next time I'll bite off your nasty tongue." He tipped his head back and to one side, as if to get a better angle of her face. "Truce?"

Before she could answer, someone called to him from the stage. "Miss Gale would like to see you in her dressing room, Dane."

With a sigh he loosened his hold and let Pet stand free. "I'll be right there," he replied. Reaching around, he took the cup of coffee from Andy and gave it back to Pet. As he walked past the refreshment table on his way backstage, he stopped to take two sugar cubes out of their box and tossed them to her. "Put some sugar in your coffee — it might sweeten your disposition."

Sheer reflex enabled her to catch them. "I haven't been the one snapping at everybody all day." She tossed them back, surprised she could move or speak.

"Women!" Dane turned away with a wry shake of his head.

Pet had the feeling she had just been lumped into a category labeled "Impossible." Warily, her gaze flashed around the semicircle of men, almost daring them to make a comment.

Joe Wiles was the only brave one. "If you're going to dish it out, Pet, you'd better learn to take it," he advised.

"I can take it," she insisted, and gulped down a swallow of tepid coffee.

But the crew was careful not to tease her about the kiss. Ten minutes later Claude was summoning them back to work.

The next day was Friday. Ruby Gale's concert was scheduled for that evening at nine o'clock. Since they were taping it before the live audience, the production crew had the morning and the bulk of the afternoon off.

Dressing for the taping that evening, Pet chose the dressier biscuit-colored slacks and a peach crepe-de-chine blouse and wrapped a brown braided rope belt around her waist. Her everyday work garb was too casual to wear in front of the public, and a dress or skirt was out of the question since she still had to climb off and on the platform.

The audience began arriving at the Garden State Arts Center half an hour before the performance was scheduled to begin. Perched on her platform in the center aisle, Pet became the cynosure of many eyes that had nothing better to do than look around while waiting for the show to start. It was amusing to listen to some of the comments.

A young brunette about her own age pointed Pet out to her date. "Look, there's a woman operating that camera."

Her date had a typical chauvinistic reply. "She's probably only a helper."

A few stopped to ask questions, most of them concerned about when the show would be seen on television. "I don't know the air date," was Pet's stock answer. "Probably in the fall or winter."

Sometimes they asked where she had learned to operate the camera. "I went to college and took courses in it."

In a way, the most difficult question to answer was why she wanted to be a cameraman. "It's what I always wanted to do," rarely satisfied them.

As the time drew closer to nine o'clock, Dane's voice came over her headset. She had barely seen him at all since yesterday's episode. The few times she had, he had been in conversation with someone else and she didn't receive any more than a preoccupied glance. In the interim, Pet thought she had got things back in their proper perspective — until she heard his voice and her pulse went skittering all over the place. His initial comments were instructions to the crew in general, then he was directing a remark solely to her. "What about you, camera two? Do you think you have the sequence of the opening number down pat?" There was a certain drollness to his tone that implied inoffensive mockery.

"If I don't, I'm sure you'll tell me about it," she replied with surprising ease.

"You can bet on it," he chuckled softly.

"I would, but nobody will give me odds," Pet returned, joking with him.

"Watch your mouth, girl, unless you want another lesson in keeping it shut." It was a mock threat, issued with a smile in his voice that made light of yesterday's incident as if it had been all in good fun.

"Promises, promises," she faked a sigh. "That's all you men ever do — promise and forget to follow through."

"I'll remember that," he warned. Then it was back to business. "Claude, how are things moving backstage?"

"We'll be on time," the floor director promised.

"Baxter, I want you to get me plenty of audience shots," Dane instructed Lon, who had the hand-held camera. "You shouldn't have any trouble when the houselights are up. The rest of the time there should be enough light falling back on the first two or three rows to give me reaction shots, not just applause."

"Gotcha, boss."

Precisely at nine the curtain went up. Right from the opening number the first half of the show went without a hitch. The mistakes by both crew and performers were so few and minor they were practically nonexistent. It seemed that all the rehearsing, the countless takes, the endless criticisms had all paid off to achieve near perfection.

Ruby Gale's performance had been electric, charged by the applauding audience. She was sexy, stunning, scintillating, alive as Pet had never seen her before. Everything flowed with such magic that when intermission arrived Pet couldn't help wondering what would happen when the clock struck twelve and the coach became a pumpkin again. Would the spell wear off?

"Excuse me, miss." An elderly man was standing beside her platform. Pet had noticed him before since he was sitting in one of the aisle seats near her position.

She shifted the mike wand of her headset away from her lips. "Yes?" She thought he probably wanted direction to the men's room. She supposed she could always ask Andy or Charlie.

"I've been watching you and I just wanted to say that you're a very beautiful woman," he said, smiling quite benignly. "You belong in front of the camera instead of behind it."

"Thank you." Her smile was wide and wholly natural.

"I know you're busy, but I just wanted to tell you that." He nodded in a gesture of apology and turned to go back to his seat.

"What did that man want?" Charlie asked, having seen the man stop to talk to her from his camera position. "Did he want you to go out with him?"

"He was very sweet," she insisted. "He told me I was beautiful and belonged in *front* of the camera."

Dane joined the conversation to state unequivocally, "Well, you don't. You belong *behind* the camera."

"That's a pleasant switch," she drawled.

"Why?" he demanded.

"Most men think women belong in a kitchen either in *front* of a stove or *behind* a sink full of dirty dishes," Pet explained in wry amusement.

"Better you than me," Dane returned in a mocking underbreath, then crisply. "Okay, gang, we have five minutes. Five minutes!"

As Pet had feared, the second half of the show didn't run as smoothly as the first. Midway through the second number, camera three went out. They had to do some fast improvisations of camera angles to cover the shots assigned to Charlie. When the problem defied immediate rectifying, the spare camera was hurriedly carted in and mounted.

In all, camera three was out for three songs, an amazingly short period. Yet that frantic race for time had thrown everyone off tempo and they were never able to regain that effortless coordination that had made the first half of the show so flawless.

It was a relief when the concert was over and the tape stopped rolling. While the audience filed out, the crew began shutting down the equipment. It was twenty minutes after the last curtain call before Pet had finished.

"Are you driving back to the hotel with me?" Charlie called to her from across the seats.

"Yeah! But I left my bag in the van," she explained. "I'll run out and get it now. Wait for me!"

The seventy-foot-long semitrailer had seemed the safest place to leave her bag during the taping. She couldn't have kept it with her on the platform since it could have been stolen too easily. Nor had it seemed wise to leave it backstage with so many people coming and going all the time.

As she walked in front of the stage, a woman stepped out from behind the curtains. Pet had seen her before. She was usually a part of Ruby Gale's personal entourage. Pet suspected she was a secretary or something.

"Excuse me," the woman requested Pet's attention with an uplifted finger. "Could you tell me where I could find Mr. Kingston?"

"I —" Pet glanced around the theater "— haven't seen him. He might still be in the trailer outside. I'm on my way out there. Shall I send him in?"

The woman considered that, then said, "Could you give him a message?"

"Sure," Pet nodded.

"Miss Gale is leaving now for her hotel. She wanted to remind him about the party she's having in her suite tonight. Would you mention it to him? Miss Gale is most anxious that he should come," the woman added.

"I'll remind him," Pet promised.

"Hurry up, Pet!" Charlie shouted.

With a quick wave to acknowledge that she had heard him, she hurried out through a side exit to where the van was parked. Its long white-painted sides gleamed in the moonlight, emblazoned with the Kingston crest and the letters spelling out Kingston Productions. A bare light bulb illuminated the metal steps leading to the side door.

As Pet reached for the railing to climb them, the door opened and Dane stepped out. He frowned in surprise when he saw her, his gaze narrowing at her haste.

"Is something wrong?" He was down the steps and grabbing her shoulders almost before she could catch her breath. "Has something happened?"

"No, I. . . ." She was momentarily flustered by his touch. "I left my handbag in the van and Charlie's waiting to give me a lift to the hotel."

"Oh." He seemed to smile at his overreaction, and let his hands fall from her shoulders. "You'd better hurry, then. If he's ready to leave, he's probably getting impatient."

"He is." She started up the steps, brushing past him, before she remembered the message she had promised to deliver. "Oh, Dane, I forgot." She stopped and half turned, unconsciously using his given name.

"What did you forget?" He moved back within the circle of light cast by the bare bulb. There was something warm and velvety in his look that tugged at her heart.

"I think it was Miss Gale's secretary. She asked me to remind you about the party Miss Gale is having in her suite tonight," Pet explained.

"Damn!" He released a long, tired breath and rubbed his forehead. Both his sound and his action made it plain he wasn't overjoyed by the message.

Pet watched him, feeling a little glad that he didn't look happy about going. "She also said Miss Gale was most anxious for you to come," she added.

"I don't have any choice," Dane said wryly. "It's more or less obilgatory on both sides. Ruby has invited some of the local dignitaries and the press over for drinks. It's good public relations — and good publicity. It's good for her, and for this television special of mine," he explained. "It's one of those business affairs masquerading as a social event."

Pet wasn't exactly sure why he was telling her this. It wasn't really any of her business what this party was for or why he felt obligated to attend. But the fact that he had made her feel . . . well, a little important.

"That's often the case in the entertainment business, I've heard," she offered in sympathy.

"Have you ever been to one of these parties?" Dane asked, tipping his head to one side and smiling faintly.

"Heavens, no!" she laughed.

"Why don't you come with me tonight?" he suggested. "Then you'll always know what you're not missing."

For a minute she thought he was serious, then she wasn't sure. "You don't want me along." She shook her head, her long blond hair swinging loose about her shoulders, and started to climb the last steps to the van door.

"I wouldn't have asked if I didn't want you

come with me, Pet." His voice was low and almost deadly serious.

Startled, she looked back. There wasn't a hint of mockery or amusement in his roughly hewn features. His look was silently questioning as he patiently waited for her answer.

"But I'm not dressed for a party. . . ." Pet managed a faint protest to give him a chance to back out of the invitation if he wanted to.

"As you can see, neither am I." He lifted his hands in a gesture to indicate the casualness of his beige silk shirt and brown slacks. "But I'm going like this. And they can hardly turn you away when you're with me. Are you coming? It will be a new experience for you. I can't say it will be one you'll want to repeat, but —"

"I'll never know, though —" she began.

"That's right," he agreed.

"Okay," Pet accepted, and shrugged, trying to be as offhand about the invitation as he was. "Why not?"

But she knew precisely why she was accepting. She wasn't at all curious about what the party might be like, nor the experience of it. It was the chance to spend a couple of hours with him that she was accepting. It was crazy, and probably foolish, but that was the truth.

"Go get your bag, I'll wait here for you," Dane said, and rested an arm on the railing at the bottom step.

The word "wait" reminded her. "Charlie's

107

waiting for me. He thinks I'm going back to the hotel."

"I'll tell him to leave without you, that you'll be with me. The gang will really be confused then," he grinned. "I'll meet you here."

"Okay," she agreed.

When she opened the trailer door, Dane had disappeared into the semidarkness. Pet didn't understand this spell he had cast over her. One minute she was infuriated with him, and in the next he could have her melting in his arms. It didn't make sense, but she wasn't sure if it had to.

Her bag was right where she had left it, tucked under the bench seat inside the door. She glanced once at the multitude of television monitors across the control panel, the screens glassy and gray, all the little lights out. Behind the panel, out of sight behind the partition, was the sophisticated computer that controlled everything and turned the semitrailer van into a portable television studio, complete with all the latest electronic gear. Pet shuddered to think how much it cost, or how wealthy that made Dane, since he owned it.

Chapter Six

A powerful sports-model Jaguar made short work of the drive to the star's hotel. Pet was surprised at how easy it had been to talk shop with Dane, as easy as it was to chat with the boys in the crew. Of course, his knowledge was far more encompassing than hers. Perhaps that was what had made his comments all the more interesting and thought-provoking.

Things she had previously regarded only from the production side, she now began to consider from the management and executive side. She had learned a great deal. She was almost sorry when Dane guided her out of the elevator and down the hallway to Ruby Gale's suite, because it meant their private conversation was coming to an end.

Gradually she realized the reason for her regret was more subtle than that. Discussing television kept her from thinking about Dane as a male escort. She had been using the talk as a defense mechanism to keep that sense of physical attraction at bay.

She realized it while they were standing in the hallway at the door to the suite, waiting for Dane's knock to be answered. His hand had found the curve of her waist, his palm covering her hipbone. The warmth of his touch was melting through her clothes to her skin, heating her flesh with an awareness of him.

Under the sweep of her lashes she slid him a look out of the corner of her eye. His roughly sculpted profile caught at her breath, disrupting its evenness. She was struck again by his height, something she didn't notice about most men since they generally weren't so much taller than she was.

As if he felt her eyes upon him, Dane's gaze swept down on her in a lazy caress that upset her heartbeat. She quivered all over inside with the desire to have him make love to her. It was faintly shocking to be so completely aroused by just a look. In delightful agitation she averted her gaze to the door, her ivory-smooth features hinting at this inner disturbance through the fluttering of her lashes and the tilting of her chin.

Dane's hand applied slight pressure on her hipbone as if he wanted to pull her closer. "You look very lovely," he murmured, and she guessed the reassurance was intended to eradicate any nervousness about her appearance. But how could she explain that a Dior gown wouldn't change the physical reaction erupting from his nearness?

"Thank you." It was a breathy answer, barely audible.

With excellent timing, the door was opened to the suite by the same woman who had given Pet the message for Dane. The polite smile she gave Dane faltered when she saw Pet with him. "Good evening, Mr. Kingston. Miss Gale will be so glad you could come."

"Hello, Clancy." There was a ghost of mockery in the look he gave the officious brunette. "You remember Miss Wallis, don't you?" he prompted as he swept Pet along with him inside the suite.

"Of course." Behind the polite nod, it was obvious the woman was trying to figure out what Pet was doing with Dane. "Miss Gale is —" The woman took a step, obviously intending to take them to their hostess.

"I see her, Clancy," Dane interrupted, glancing across the room.

Ruby Gale's red hair was a beacon, standing out in the crowd of people, mostly men. Pet had spied her almost instantly, too, but mostly she was staring at the decor of the suite. It boggled the imagination.

Pink. Everywhere there were shades of pink from the thick, powder-puff carpet to the rose velvet sofas and chairs. On nearly every other antiqued-white tabletop there were vases of flowers, mainly dark pink roses. White woodwork outlined the pastel print silk covering the walls. Even the caterers were wearing dark rose red jackets over black trousers. Pet felt as if she was gawking as Dane guided her into the main room of the suite.

Removing two glasses of champagne from a proffered tray, he pressed one into her hand,

111

and her gaze flickered to his face in faint surprise. Amusement glittered openly in his velvet brown eyes at her stunned reaction to the room. She let her gaze sweep around it again before lifting the glass to sip the bubbling wine.

"I thought hotel suites like this existed only in Hollywood movies," she commented.

"It's horrendous, isn't it?" he agreed, keeping his voice low, too. "You should see the main bedroom. It has a round bed with a red velvet canopy draped into a rose design. I think I prefer mirrors to staring at giant red roses above my head."

A sick feeling weighted Pet's stomach. Was he speaking from experience? Of course he was. She was angry with herself for even questioning it. How else would he have known about the bed unless he'd lain in it? Only a completely naive fool would believe he had only been testing the mattress for firmness. And she wasn't naive. She had always suspected — known — that he and Ruby were lovers, so why had she accepted his invitation to this party? The answer was so plainly simple. She had a fatal fascination for this sexy, exciting man who could enrage or arouse her by turns.

This inability to resist him made her feel spineless. She took another sip of champagne, wildly hoping the effervescent spirits would temporarily stiffen her backbone. The constricting muscles in her throat rejected it with a tiny choking cough.

"I'm surprised the champagne isn't pink," she managed at last, her long fingers delicately covering her lips.

"Ruby probably didn't think of it." A smile twitched the corners of Dane's mouth as his gaze ran interestedly over her face, a little aloof. "I told you this would be an experience. You find it distasteful, don't you?"

There were many things she found distasteful, mainly the discovery that she was envious of Ruby Gale for the time she had spent with Dane in that round bed with the rose canopy. Although her features were schooled not to reveal her feelings, her expressive sea-green eyes obviously reflected them for Dane to see. Since he had misguessed the cause, she didn't choose to enlighten him.

"This suite, it's all so phony." Pet shrugged to show her dislike of it, lowering her gaze to the sparkling liquid in the crystal wineglass.

Dane's fingers touched her cheek to turn her face to him, then moved away. "And you aren't, are you?" He studied her more closely as if discovering something he hadn't noticed before.

Pet became uneasy under his scrutiny and immediately Dane ended it, shifting his gaze to the room of people, buzzing with hearty conversations that rang false.

"This is all part of the image," he said, a sweeping glance encompassing everything. "All of these people would have been disappointed and disillusioned if this suite had turned out to be no different from any they could have rented for one night. Ruby Gale is a star. Nothing ordinary would suit her — in their eyes. A star deserves to be surrounded by a spectacle. Ruby is smart. She gives them what they want. It keeps them coming back for more."

His narrowed gaze drifted back to Pet. She wondered if that explanation was true for him, as well. "It's fake, a fantasy world of red-hots and candy canes — sugar and spice wrapped up in glitter and sequins. It's called packaging the product."

"I suppose that's true," Pet conceded with a trace of his cynicism.

"You haven't been formally introduced to the 'product,' have you?" Dane remembered, and closed a hand on her elbow. "We'd better correct that omission before Ruby starts throwing real poisonous darts instead of invisible ones."

Following the direction of his callously amused glance, Pet saw their hostess through a gap in the duster of guests. Her long hair was about her white shoulders in a mass of titian curls. The daringly cut spangled gown was the same peacock-blue shade as her eyes — eyes that glittered with impatience and irritation whenever they rested on Dane, which was often.

When Dane and Pet had weaved their way through the crowd to the star's side, Ruby Gale gave Dane one of her radiantly provocative smiles. "I wondered when you were going to

114

show up, darling," she chided him playfully for his tardiness, and curved a scarlet-nailed hand along the back of his neck when he bent to greet her with a kiss.

Their lips clung together a few seconds longer than the length of a merely casual kiss. Pet was prepared for the violent surge of rage that shook her. She stood motionless, her face frozen into blankness, while the three men Ruby had been speaking to exchanged knowing glances and raised eyebrows.

When Dane lifted his head, the star wiped the traces of lipstick from his mouth with her fingers.

The gesture, more than the kiss, implied a long-standing familiarity and intimacy between them. It was also possessive. Pet was rigidly aware that Dane didn't protest against any of it.

Then the redhead was linking both her arms though the crook of his elbow, further staking her claim to him while turning to the trio she was with. "You all know Dane Kingston — my producer, my director, my —" Ruby paused deliberately, sweeping him a look through her long lashes as if exchanging a secret "— dear friend."

The phrase drew a faint smile from Dane, which made a total mockery of it. Pet would have slipped away, but he chose that moment to remember she was with him and turned to take her hand, drawing her within the circle. She half expected to be murdered by Ruby's blue eyes, but they seemed blank of expression when they regarded her. Her burgundy-glossed lips were parted in a welcoming smile of interest.

"I don't believe I know this young woman, do I, Dane?" she asked, and extended an open hand to Pet.

Pet let her hand be clasped warmly by the star and even managed a stiff smile. Pride kept her head high while a defensiveness masked her gaze with a wary coolness.

"How do you do, Miss Gale," she greeted the redhead with exaggerated politeness.

"You haven't actually met her before, Ruby," Dane explained. "But you have spent the last few days looking at her without knowing it. This is Petra Wallis. She's been operating the number-two camera."

"The center one?" Now the star's gaze became sharp, slicing Pet into unimportant pieces. "You actually have a woman in sole charge of a camera? I didn't realize you were so liberated in your views, Dane. You've never exhibited that tendency before."

"Haven't I? Maybe you just never noticed," he suggested, turning aside the comment.

"Are you his token female, Miss Wallis?" the star inquired archly. In explanation to the other men, Ruby Gale defended her question. "With all these new laws nowadays about hiring women for traditionally male jobs, it's almost mandatory for an employer to hire a woman if she applies for a position. Me, I'm not in favor at all of this new equality for women. I love being the weaker sex, and dominated by a big, strong man." Her glance at Dane made it obvious who that "big, strong man" was.

Pet seethed with jealousy and the sensation of betrayal by one of her own kind. What Ruby Gale was insinuating was insulting and demeaning to her. Worse, the three men with their glasses of champagne and lascivious looks were nodding agreement with Ruby Gale's remarks.

"I can assure you that I wasn't forced to hire Miss Wallis," Dane inserted lazily. "Her sex had nothing to do with her employment. I doubt if it was even taken into consideration by anyone in the company."

His support didn't bring the reassurance that it should have. Instead, one of the younger men — a reporter by the cynical look of him — gave Pet an assessing look that stripped her quite naked. Anger flashed in her eyes, the turbulent green of storm-tossed seas.

"I certainly could never interview you, Miss Wallis, without being conscious of your sex," he remarked suggestively, and everyone chuckled in total agreement.

Pet struggled to contain her anger. Usually she could ignore such biased and prejudiced remarks from men, dismissing them as small remarks from small minds. Yet she was bristling from them.

"It's a shame that employers are forced by law to hire incompetent help. It's so expensive in the long run," Ruby Gale was saying, and turned to Dane. "Just look at all the delays and technical problems we encountered taping this concert simply because of one or two unskilled members of the crew."

"As a professional, Ruby, you know there are always problems of one kind or another," Dane stated with a hard glint in his eyes. "But you certainly can't blame Miss Wallis. She's the best technician in the company — that's why I put her on camera two. When you're on center stage you deserve to have the best covering you, so I made certain you had it. You'll see for yourself when we review the tapes of tonight's performance."

"My, my!" The redhead blinked her startling blue eyes and teased him with a smile. "Such praise coming from you, Dane!" Her gaze shifted to Pet, who had been stunned and skeptical of his assertive defense. "You must be very flattered."

"I am," she admitted, since flattery also implied exaggeration.

"Is that why you brought Miss Wallis to the party? As a reward for all her work?" Ruby questioned, and rose on tiptoe to kiss his cheek. "How sweet of you, darling! You really are very thoughtful."

The conclusion Ruby had reached sent Pet's mind racing. Was that the explanation for this unexpected invitation? Was she to regard her attendance at this party as a bonus for a job well done? She had liked it better when she believed it was just a friendly invitation.

"I'm not certain if Pet would agree with you, Ruby," Dane commented, and sent a roguish glance in her direction. "I think she's convinced I'm a cross between an ogre and a tyrant."

"You neglected to mention an interfering busybody," Pet reminded him smoothly.

"So I did," he agreed, and lifted his champagne glass in wry acknowledgement of the omission.

"What's this all about?" Ruby glanced from one to the other, suspicion shimmering in her hard blue eyes.

"A minor rebellion in the ranks against authority." Dane dismissed their previous skirmishes with an indifferent shrug of a shoulder and sipped at his wine. "I neglected to tell you how sensational you were this evening, Ruby. You had the audience in the palm of your beautiful hand all the time."

Diverted by his compliment, the redhead beamed, "Thank you, darling."

"Hear, hear," one of the men murmured in agreement, and lifted his glass in a silent toast to her successful performance.

"Yes, to a very triumphant performance by our own Jersey Lily." A second man made it a verbal salute.

"In case you men haven't noticed it, your star

is a tiger lily — a wild, exotic flower," Dane remarked with an admiring glance running warmly over the titian-haired entertainer.

Pet could almost see the reporter making a mental note of the phrase. She was certain it would show up somewhere in the postperformance publicity.

"You know all the right things to say to make a woman feel special, Dane," Ruby purred, and let her hand glide along his arm to curl her fingers through his. "I should be upset with you for bringing a blond to my private party, but here I am — putty in your hands."

"Never putty," he denied, and lifted her fingers to his mouth with continental ease. "Rare blue clay, maybe."

Her faint laugh was a low, throaty sound. "I never know whether to believe you. I guess that's part of your dangerous charm," the star suggested. For once, Pet was in total agreement with the red-haired performer, regarding her assessment of Dane Kingston.

Ruby slipped her hand out of the loose clasp of his fingers. "But I really must circulate, darling. You're making me neglect my guests. Be sure to introduce . . . Miss Wallis around."

"I will," he replied smoothly.

Pet had the distinct impression that Ruby Gale had given him permission to escort her. It would have proved more bolstering to her self-esteem if the star had resented Dane's accompanying her. This way the woman obviously didn't regard her as representing a serious threat.

The three men introduced themselves, but Pet didn't make an effort to remember their names. Dane chatted with them a few minutes, then took Pet by the arm to wander to another group. The procedure was repeated several times, and Pet realized that Dane was doing his own brand of circulating, advertising his product and making himself known to those who were important. A necessary part of any business was socializing.

But she had a great deal of difficulty relaxing in his company. She could talk quite naturally with others, yet could manage only a stiff nod or some stilted reply when Dane addressed a remark to her. Tension began drumming at her temples, demanding a respite from the constant strain of his presence.

A particularly garrulous guest had trapped Dane into a conversation about the merits of the present television programming, and Pet took the opportunity to touch his arm lightly to briefly claim his attention.

"Excuse me, I'm going to freshen my lipstick. I'll only be a few moments," she murmured as his gaze wandered over her mouth to assess the need.

Without waiting for his permission, Pet moved away. The brunette secretary whom Dane had addressed as Clancy showed her where the ladies' powder room was located in the suite, and Pet sank onto the strawberry velvet stool in front of the lighted mirror and gazed at her reflection.

A pair of plain gold studs gleamed on the lobes of her ears. The sides of her long hair were pulled high on the crown of her head and secured with a wide gold barrette. Strong, mat-smooth features were sculpted in clean, pure lines of classical symmetry rather than pretti-ness. With its jade eyes, it was an arresting face that would wear well.

Pet saw the absence of raw sensuality and an-imation. Noting the pallor of her lips, she re-moved the tube of gloss from her bag and outlined her mouth with the burgundy stick. She ran a comb through the ends of her hair and flipped it down the center of her back. With a sigh she accepted the fact that her cool blond sophistication was no competition for the earthy appeal of the auburn temptress.

Entering the spacious main room of the suite, she spied Dane with a state politician, and the independent streak in her asserted itself. In-stead of making her way to his side, she wan-dered over to the hors d'oeuvres table, sampled some caviar, which she loved, and stuffed mushroom buttons, then accepted another glass of champagne.

"It's quite an affair, isn't it?" a cynical male voice remarked to the right of her elbow.

Turning her head, Pet glanced down at the man easily three inches shorter than she was.

She resisted the age-old impulse to hunch her shoulders, an impossibility with the thin shoulder pads under her peach silk blouse. The man was familiar, but it was a second before she remembered he was one of the three who had been talking to Ruby Gale when she and Dane had joined them. At the time she had decided he was a reporter.

"Yes, it is." She continued to stand straight and tall.

"Petra Wallis, isn't it?" he remembered her name.

"Either you have an excellent memory or else you know everyone else here," Pet replied with a wry look over the rim of her champagne glass.

"It's a combination," he admitted. "I know most of the people who are here, remembering names is part of my trade, and a man would be a fool to forget yours."

He smiled for the first time without some inner cynicism. In his late thirties, he wasn't really an unattractive man without that expression of bored superiority. Plain brown hair and shrewd brown eyes went with his unassuming features. As his gaze made a thorough study of her, it didn't contain the suggestive stripping quality that he had subjected her to before. Pet didn't feel any of the initial hostility he had generated in their earlier meeting.

"I know you've probably forgotten. The name is Nick Brewster." He wasn't offended that she had.

"You're with the newspaper, right?" She wasn't sure if she had been told or if it was only a guess.

"Yeah, I'm doing a feature article on the 'Tiger Lily' for the entertainment section. I'll probably send it around — syndicate it to a few other papers." He shrugged to hide the boasting tone, then studied her again. "You might have given me an idea on a different angle."

"Me?" Pet was startled.

"Yeah. The star through the eyes of a television camera." He made an imaginary frame with his hands.

"I'm not sure that I understand what you mean." She shook her head, vaguely confused.

"I'd be writing it from your viewpoint," the journalist explained. "What Ruby Gale is like to work with, that kind of thing. You've seen her in rehearsal and in concert. How is she different?"

"That's easy. Before an audience she's electric. When she's rehearsing, she's concentrating on technique, delivery, the routine." Pet didn't see how that was particularly interesting or new.

"But what about her temperament? Is she congenial to work with? Demanding?"

She began to see where his questions were leading. "Naturally she's demanding — of herself and everyone else."

"Come on, Miss Wallis, you can tell me."

The reporter eyed her with a mocking yet confiding look. "It's common knowledge that she can be a temperamental bitch, throwing tantrums, walking off the stage. From some of the things I've overheard, this last session hasn't been without its problems."

"Of course we've had some problems," Pet admitted. "But I haven't seen any evidence of this temper you're describing."

He raised a skeptical eyebrow. "Dane must have her eating out of his hand!" When Pet showed signs of becoming aloof, he chided her. "Everyone knows that the two of them are having an affair. They aren't trying to hide it, even if he did drag you here."

"I wouldn't presume to discuss Mr. Kingston's private life with you, even if I were privy to any of that kind of information — which I'm not," she retorted. "I'm an employee, nothing more."

"Such loyalty!" he mocked her, his gaze sliding sideways. "It should be rewarded, Mr. Kingston. But I forgot," he pretended as Pet turned to find Dane standing near her elbow, "this invitation to the party was by way of a reward."

"You should ask who's being rewarded, Mr. Brewster." Dane smiled pleasantly and laced his fingers through hers. "Maybe the pleasure of Miss Wallis's company is my compensation for a week of hard work and long hours."

"I wouldn't be surprised," the reporter

laughed. "Some people can have their cake and eat it, too."

"Then you won't mind if I don't share. Excuse us."

Dane led Pet away. The smile faded from his expression, if it had ever really been there at all, and his dark gaze was sharp as it examined her. "I'm sorry. I hope Brewster didn't subject you to too much of his dirty digging."

"He didn't." She was curt as she pulled her hand free from him. She disliked being used as a red herring. "Not that it matters. I'm not in the habit of airing other people's dirty linen, even if I had possession of it — which I don't."

"What's that supposed to mean?" Impatience clipped his voice.

"It means that I didn't have any 'dirt' to give him," Pet shrugged with feigned indifference and refused to meet his gaze.

"He did upset you," he concluded grimly.

"He didn't," she insisted. If she was upset, it was because of the round bed with the rose canopy, Dane's insincere praise of her skill, the nonthreat she was to Ruby Gale and the farcical invitation to this party. "I have been around television and news reporters before. I didn't need to be rescued."

"I can't win with you, can I?" Dane sighed with thinly disguised anger. "I try to do a good deed and I'm accused of meddling again."

"Is that my fault?" Pet countered defensively.

"I had hoped for a pleasant evening, not another one of our verbal matches of word slinging." The reply was underlined with tautness.

On that, Pet agreed. "Perhaps we're both tired. It's been a long, tension-filled evening in many respects." She was thinking of more than the taping.

"Yes." But there was a grim reluctance in his acceptance of her explanation. "We'd better make our apologies to Ruby and leave."

Without waiting for her reply, he cupped a hand under her elbow and guided her to the corner of the room where the flame-haired woman was flirting with one of the several politicians in attendance.

"Darling!" When Ruby Gale saw Dane, she must have read his intention in his face. "You're not leaving so soon?"

"We must," he said firmly, and sent an aloofly apologetic glance to the others for having interrupted them. Smoothly, he bent forward to kiss an artfully rouged cheek.

"I suppose you must," Ruby sighed, and let her glittering blue eyes wander to Pet. "After all, Miss Wallis is a working girl." The tone seemed to relegate Pet to an inferior class. "Call me tomorrow, darling. But not too early."

"It probably won't be until the afternoon. I'll be busy in the morning," Dane replied.

"Good evening, Miss Gale," Pet inserted so she wouldn't be ignored or treated as if she weren't there.

"Good evening, Miss Wallis." The phrase was returned, but most indifferently.

Then Dane's hand was on her waist, guiding her away toward the door. When the stocky secretary appeared Dane dismissed her with a brisk, "We can find our own way out. Good night, Clancy."

"Good night, Mr. Kingston."

Chapter Seven

The silence between them was almost tangible, charging the air with crackling undercurrents. Not a word had been spoken since they had left Ruby Gale's hotel. Pet sat motionless in the bucket seat, an arm resting on the padded upholstery covering the door, a hand covering her mouth while she stared out of the side window of the car.

She ached inside — ached for the pleasure that could have been. If things had been different! But they hadn't. The evening had been a disastrous experience. She would rather have not discovered how deeply attracted she was to Dane Kingston, how jealous she could be and how easily hurt. The one consolation was that such intensity couldn't last; it would burn itself out. She had only to wait. In the meantime it was sweet agony to be sitting beside this vitally male member of the opposite sex, and forcing herself to ignore him.

In an empty parking stall next to the side entrance of the motel, Dane braked the car to a stop and switched off the powerful engine. Feeling his gaze burrowing into her, Pet collected the leather handbag from her lap and reached for the door handle, but Dane was quicker, leaning over to seize her wrist and prevent her escape. His arm was an iron band running diagonally across her, the sensitive nerve ends in her breast aware of every rippling outline of his muscles beneath the silken material of his shirt sleeve.

"What's bothering you, Pet?" His voice was low and taut with command.

Her head turned away from the door to bring him into her side vision, but she didn't look at him. She was conscious of the hard cast of his features, the determined grimness in the set of his jaw, and the harshness of his thin mouth.

"Nothing's bothering me," she insisted in cool dismissal.

"Something is," Dane persisted, not relaxing his hold so she could open the door. "And I don't believe it had anything to do with that reporter Brewster anymore. You were acting like this before he cornered you."

"I don't know what you're talking about," Pet lied in a weary breath. "I'm tired, so will you please let go of my hand? I'd like to go to my room and get some rest."

For a long second she didn't think Dane was going to release her. A barrage of suffocating sensations closed in on her. The air was warmly thick with the male scent unique to him, spiced with a whiff of his after-shave lotion. Under his muscled arm her heart was drumming its panic, while her flesh quivered ecstatically beneath his touch.

Then the talon-hard grip of her wrist was

loosened and the restricting band of his arm was removed, setting her free. She sensed the impatience and irritation in his action, just as if he knew he could have obtained a truthful answer if he had pursued it. She was grateful he hadn't as she climbed out of the sports car. Simultaneously the door was slammed on the driver's side.

The summer night air was refreshingly cool against her heated face. Dane was waiting on the sidewalk to walk with her to the side entrance of the hotel, his eyes never relaxing their inspection of her until she was at his side. Pet held her head unnaturally high, keeping her face empty of expression.

Dane made no attempt to touch her, no guiding hand touched her arm or waist as they walked. There was something aloofly mocking in the way he held the door open for her to enter the building first, a tinge of smoldering anger in his brown eyes.

When they reached her room door, Pet already had the key out of her bag but, before she could make a move to unlock the door, Dane was taking the key from her hand and turning coldly to insert it in the lock. Her pulse was racing with the memory of the last time he'd done it, and the result.

At the click of the lock, Dane pushed the door open and stepped aside. The key was in his hand, yet he seemed hesitant to return it to her, as if he, too, was remembering the last time. She held her breath for those few seconds. When he started to hand it to her, she knew she had to say something to him before going inside.

"Thank you for a lovely evening," she coolly recited the meaningless phrase that was intended to dismiss him.

A savage anger darkened his expression. "Don't pawn that polite garbage off on me!" he rejected it with a low snarl. "It was a lousy evening and we both know it."

"All right, it was!" Pet agreed sharply, reacting to his anger out of self-defense. She forgot about the key in her need to get inside the room and shut the door on him.

Before she could succeed, his outstretched arm had stiffened to keep the door jammed open. "I want to know why," he demanded.

The hollow wood door seemed an inadequate shield against the man filling its frame and bracing it open with an arm. Yet Pet stood partially behind it, taking advantage of whatever protection it offered. The silken material of his beige shirt was stretched across his male physique, outlining his muscled torso and intimidating her with the contained strength that lay beneath it.

"Maybe I don't like being patronized!" she flared. "Did that ever occur to you?"

He shoved the door all the way open, pushing her backward as if her weight against it were no more of a deterrent than a feather. His long stride carried him past the door.

"You're going to explain that remark!" he snapped, stopping before she felt threatened enough to retreat in the face of his advance.

With a backward push of his hand he sent the door swinging shut, although it didn't latch, only fell closed in its frame. His hands were on his hips, his stance challenging. Pet found the strength to confront him with all the many wounds to her pride she had endured that night.

"For starters, I didn't appreciate those absurdly flattering things you told Ruby Gale about me," she retorted.

"What things?" He looked taken aback, startled confusion entering his harsh frown.

"You know very well what things!" Pet stormed. "Those ridiculous lies that I was the best cameraman in the group! If you felt you had to defend me and rationalize my presence for her benefit, you could have simply said I was good. You didn't have to insult me with all that false praise!"

Her voice was choking on the last. Conscious of the sting of bitter tears pricking her eyes, she pivoted before he noticed, intending to put distance between them, but Dane grabbed her arm and spun her back.

"False praise!" he exploded.

"Yes!" She twisted her arm, trying to pull it out of his hold, but his fingers tightened to dig into her flesh.

"You little fool, that happened to be the truth," he muttered through clenched teeth.

"Oh, come on now!" Pet derisively mocked him. "I should have made a tape recording of the cross talk." That was the term for the communication over the headsets. "Some of your rebukes were positively scathing!"

When she tried to walk away, Dane turned her back and pinned her shoulders to the wall. "You're not going anywhere," he informed her roughly. "You're going to stay right here and listen to me!"

"I'm not interested in hearing any more of your lies!" But she didn't have any choice. His arms were the bars trapping her between the wall and his towering frame.

"Then listen to reason," he demanded, and brought his face close to hers, his tanned features etched with fierce determination and suppressed anger. "You must have some small idea of how much money I have wrapped up in this special. Do you think that I chose this production crew at random? Every member I personally handpicked, because I wanted the best! And that includes you! I've reviewed everything you've done. I knew I was borrowing trouble by bringing a single woman on location — a *beautiful* single woman, I might add. But trouble or not, I'd have the best. That's why you're here, so what I told Ruby wasn't a lie."

His explanation made sense, but Pet couldn't relate it to the way he'd treated her these past few days. She eyed him warily, distrusting her ability to sort fact from fiction where he was concerned. He simply had too much influence over her ability to reason.

"Is that what made you angry, Pet?" he questioned in a gentler tone as his gaze roamed over her face, then paused to linger on her mouth and watch it form an answer.

"You're always making me angry." That was easy to admit. "You're always saying something to irritate me."

"The next time I do," he murmured, moving closer, "why don't you try kissing me? I guarantee it will shut me up."

Bending his head, he took her lips. Pet stood very still, inwardly shaking with the desire to put her arms around him, but she permitted her hands to go no farther than his chest, resting lightly on his shirt and feeling the heat of his body warm her palms. His mouth moved powerfully against her own, parting her lips and invading them with a hot sweetness.

A whirl of confused sensation began taking over her body, spinning a fine web of dazzling brilliance. His hands pulled her from the wall and into the support of his arms. When his mouth grazed a path across her cheek to the lobe of her ear, Pet dipped her head against his shoulder in mute surrender, clinging to him.

"Why did you say those things?" she murmured, still not understanding that part. "Why did you make me think you believed I was incompetent?"

"I never intended you to think that." His voice was soft against her ear, his mouth brushing the cool metal of the gold stud earring. "I couldn't tolerate anything but the best from you because I knew you could give it to me. You could always give it to me."

There was the heady implication that he was referring to more than her work. His hands glided slowly over her spine to press her against his hard, lithe body. Her head was spinning as he kissed her throat and followed the wildly pulsing vein in her neck to the sensitive hollow below her ear. Then he was seeking her lips again, consuming her with his hunger. Pet struggled for some semblance of control before he undermined it completely.

"That party —" her lips were against his cheek, their moist softness scraped by the rough stubble of his beard, increasing their sensitivity "— was it a reward for doing a good job?" With each breath she inhaled the intoxicating smell of him and weaved at its potency. "Is that why you invited me?"

"That damned party was the last place I wanted to go tonight," he muttered, lifting his head to satisfy himself that she did look kissed and aroused. "But I had to go. It was as compulsory for me to attend as it was for Ruby to give it. And I knew the crew would be having a celebration of their own. If you weren't with me, you'd be with them."

"So you were just keeping me out of trouble again." Hurt, she flattened her hands against his chest, resisting, yet aware of the heavy beat of his heart.

"I wasn't looking after you." Dane shook his head wryly. "I was looking after me. You get into a man's blood, Pet. I thought I had a chance of enduring that insufferable chatter if you were with me, but it all went sour within minutes after we arrived, and I couldn't understand why. I thought you wanted to be with me as much as I wanted to be with you."

"Did you really?" She wanted to believe him, but she was afraid to. The doubt glistened in her green eyes.

"Can you doubt it?" he demanded, and crushed her lips beneath his mouth, devouring them in a rapacious assault of passion that left her breathless and dazed.

The pressure of the hand at the small of her back was fiercely possessive. She was hardly conscious of his other hand moving to stroke her hair. His fingers found the gold barrette that secured the top and sides in a single clasp at the crown. With a deft snap he unfastened it to let the silken length tumble free, and a half-muffled groan rippled from his throat as he tunneled his hand beneath the golden mass.

"I've wanted to do that for so long." His mouth formed the words against hers, roughly moving over her lips with uncontained urgency.

Desire flooded her mind and body, sweeping her high on a tide of emotion that was dizzying. In Dane's arms, held close to his hard shape, Pet forgot about the round bed and the rose canopy, and his ongoing affair with Ruby Gale. His dominating kiss could make her forget everything but this aching need for his possession, to be a part of his hard male vitality.

His shirt became an irritating barrier, keeping her from the closeness she sought. Her eager fingers found the row of buttons and began unfastening them one by one until the metal buckle of his belt stopped them. Unable to resist any longer, she slid her hands inside his shirt and over his hard, flat stomach to caress the taut skin covering his rib cage. His hand took the same license, slipping off the rope belt to glide under her blouse onto the bare skin of her back. When it moved to the front to enclose a firm breast in its palm, a searing joy quivered through her.

The loud voice singing in the hallway made little impact on her passion-charged senses, which blocked out the intrusion of noise. The crew's merrymaking had no part in her sensual revelry.

"Hey, Pet!" A loud, slurring voice remarkably resembling Lon Baxter's called her name. "Wake up! You've got to come to the party!"

The first hand to pound on the unlatched door swung it open while the combination of noise and movement cleaved their lips apart, but there wasn't any way they could untangle their hands from inside each other's clothes. In cold shock, Pet stared at Lon and the handful of other crew members clustered around her door.

Dane recovered a shade quicker than she did, withdrawing his hand from under her blouse to let it rest reassuringly on her arm. His action drew her glance, and she shuddered at the grimness in his features and the accusing silence from her co-workers.

"The door was open," someone mumbled in an attempt at an apology.

"Yeah," Lon agreed, swaying belligerently in the opening. "We wanted to invite you to our party, but you were having a little private one of your own, weren't you, Pet?"

The color that had receded from her cheeks came flooding back. She looked away from the door, pushing at the rumpled length of hair near her ear. Vaguely she was conscious of someone urging Lon to come away from the door, then Dane was letting her go to button his shirt.

"*All* the parties are over, boys," he stressed in a tired voice. "It's time we all called it a night. We have to tear down and pack the equipment first thing in the morning."

A few embarrassed mumbles of agreement followed his statement. The quiet shuffling of feet was a vast contrast to their exuberant, revel-rousing arrival as the men retreated down the hallway.

"Pet?" His quiet use of her name lifted her head. Dane was near the open door, half-turned to study her.

"You'd better leave," she said stiffly. "They'll hang around to see if you go."

"I'm aware of that," he replied dryly.

Staying close to the wall, she moved to the door and wrapped her fingers on the knob to close it while keeping a distance from him. Aftershock had started her thinking about the round bed with its giant rose canopy and a red-haired woman in his arms.

"Good night." It was a tight sound, but she accompanied it with a proud toss of her head.

Dane took a half step toward her, his mouth thinning, then stopped. "Good night."

As soon as he was in the hall, Pet closed the door and locked it. She leaned against it, her knees shaking in reaction. Across the hall she heard his door open and close, then silence.

She managed to keep her mind blank as she undressed and slipped on her nightdress. Switching off the light, she crawled under the covers of her empty bed. A few minutes earlier she wouldn't have been lying there alone, she realized, and tightly closed her eyes. The thought started a war between regret and gratitude. There wasn't a clear-cut victor by the time she fell asleep.

Firm and warm, a mouth eased itself onto her lips, gently moving over them to explore their curves. It coaxed them into a sensual pliancy, masterfully persuading a response. A sharp, masculine fragrance tingled her nose, clean, fresh and divinely heady.

What a delicious way to wake up, Pet thought as that warm mouth drifted kisses over her cheek and jaw. She arched her neck to allow access to the sensitive skin along its curve, and the mouth nibbled a slow path to the base of her throat and returned up the other side.

A soft, sensuously contented sound came from her throat, inviting that pair of masculine lips back to hers to urge a further response. Arms that had been flung above her head in sleep were lifted to find the one who was causing all these wonderful sensations. Her languorous hands encountered a muscled set of wide shoulders encased in some smooth material that allowed her to feel the contoured outline of his hard flesh.

A forearm rested on the mattress alongside her to position him above her while his other hand caressed the bare skin near the curve of her opposite shoulder. It was all so beautiful, so enchanted — like a dream that had come to life. Dane felt so solid and real, his thick springing hair curling around her fingers as she curved them to the back of his neck.

Gradually it dawned on her that the dream was real. It was all the better when she slowly lifted her lashes and saw that rugged face poised an inch above her own. Finding him sitting on her bed and kissing her awake was much too pleasant a surprise for Pet to be shocked. Her initial reaction was curiosity. She shifted her head on the pillow to get a better look at him, her gaze wandering to the lazy half curve of his mouth and her hands sliding from his back to his arms.

"How did you get in here?" she murmured with a flicker of a curious frown.

"I forgot to return your key last night. Evidently I slipped it in my pocket," he explained absently while his fingers stroked the delicate curve of her neck. "This morning I found it when I was transferring my keys and change from my brown pants to these."

"What time is it?" she wondered, rousing a bit from her delicious lethargy.

"Seven-thirty," Dane admitted, and bent his head to let his tongue trace the hollow of her throat.

For an instant Pet surrendered to the provocative sensation. Then his answer awakened alarm bells in her head. She shrank against the mattress to end the distraction of his caress.

"Is it that late?" Pet protested. "I have to be at the center by eight to help pack up the equipment."

"I know," he sighed, and lifted his head. "I stopped at the desk to leave your key. That's when I realized you'd probably forgotten to leave a wakeup call. I checked with the clerk and he verified it, so I used the key to do it personally."

"You could have used the house phone," she pointed out impishly.

"This is much more rewarding." He was so close, his mouth brushed her lips when he spoke. "I fully intended to wake up with you this morning until we were so rudely interrupted. This is the next best thing."

Pet wished he hadn't brought that up. It reminded her of the stunned and accusing expressions that had been on the faces of the boys when they had accidentally barged in on her and Dane. She knew it wasn't because they had caught her in the arms of a man. No, it was worse than that. She had been in the arms of their boss.

"You'd better let me up." She nudged him with her hands in a gentle reproof to move. "I still have to get dressed."

"I have a better idea," Dane murmured, settling more firmly into place. "Instead of you getting up, why don't I climb into bed?"

"No!" Her refusal was too quick and too weak, because she had never been exposed to a sweeter temptation in her life.

"Why not?" It wasn't a question to which he expected an answer as his mouth traveled onto her lips as soft as a wind song, and the probing point of his tongue traced their outline.

His fingers slid the strap of her nightdress off her shoulders. It immediately loosened the dark lace of the gown's bodice, allowing his hand to slide inside and cup her breast. Pet breathed in sharply in an unconscious and searing response. With masterful ease Dane explored and caressed its sensitive point into pebble hardness.

It took a concerted effort to turn her mouth away from his tantalizing kiss. "Dane, I have to go to work," she insisted tremulously.

"Have you forgotten?" He laughed softly against her throat, confident and male. "I'm the boss. I'm giving you the morning off."

"A special assignment?" She resented the use of his authority.

"If you want to call it that." He missed the hint of bitterness in her tone. "I want you, Pet. I want to make love to you." An element of urgency entered the rough pressure of his mouth against her cheek, rubbing closer to the edge of her lips. "I'll see that you're satisfied, too — I've been told I'm a good lover. But with you, Pet, I'll be even better."

He should have known it was the wrong thing to say. With a muffled cry Pet twisted from beneath him and rolled to the opposite side of the bed from where he was seated. She came quickly to her feet, grabbing the thin cotton robe draped over the end of the bed. A dark frown of confusion clouded his face.

"Who told you you were good?" Pet stormed. "Ruby Gale? While you were lying in her round bed with the giant rose overhead?"

"What the hell are you talking about?" he demanded, coming to his feet to glare at her across the width of the bed.

She hurriedly tugged the robe on. "This hotel room doesn't come equipped with mirrors on the ceiling. You'd better find yourself another room!"

"Will you make sense?" Dane exploded.

"I am making sense!" Pet retorted. "That's what makes it . . . awful!" She choked on the last and pivoted away, blinking at the tears filling her eyes.

"We aren't going to start this again," he warned.

The knock on the door was a welcome interruption. "Yes? Who is it?" Her voice was strained. She quickly wiped at the trickle of tears on her cheek.

"It's me, Lon. Aren't you awake yet?" There was a taut frown in the answer he called.

"Damn!" she cursed softly. Of all people, why did it have to be him? Or was he checking up on her because of last night? Behind her there was a faint sound from Dane that suggested similar irritation, but Pet wouldn't turn around to look.

"Yes, I'm awake," she answered back, her voice growing steadier in its volume.

"When you didn't show up for breakfast, I thought I'd better check," Lon replied in explanation of his presence. "What did you do? Oversleep?"

"Yes," Pet admitted. "Thanks for checking."

"I've brought you some coffee."

Which meant she had to open the door. She threw an anxious glance over her shoulder at Dane. His mouth was compressed in a tight, hard line, a grimly resigned expression on his features. She pushed her tousled hair away from her ear and walked reluctantly to the door, holding the front of her robe shut.

Behind her, Dane made no attempt to conceal himself from view. Lon saw him standing at the end of the bed the instant she opened the door and his gaze flashed over Pet in silent condemnation.

"I should have known why you overslept," he jeered.

"It isn't like that at all," Pet denied his conclusion in a weary voice.

"Like you, I also noticed she wasn't around," Dane inserted. "I brought her coffee, too. One cup." He lifted a Styrofoam cup to show the cameraman. "So you can lift your imagination out of the gutter."

"Listen, you may be Dane Kingston, the big man around here —" Lon stabbed an angry finger in the air adopting a belligerent stance "— but you want to crawl in bed with her the same as I do!"

Pet shivered at the cold rage that flashed across Dane's face. "I'm going to forget you said that, Baxter. Now get out!" he snapped.

"Like hell!" Lon took a step forward.

"No, please." Pet half lifted a hand to stop him. "Both of you leave. Mr. Kingston was just

146

going anyway . . . weren't you?" She cast a challenging look at Dane, her heart hammering at her ribs. The last thing she wanted was an ugly scene.

He held her gaze for a fraction of a second, then strode forward. His hard glance flicked over her as he brushed past her into the hallway occupied by Lon Baxter. There had been a promise in his look that their discussion wasn't over, merely postponed.

"I'll wait for you in the lobby, Pet," Lon stated.

She simply nodded and closed the door. Her gaze strayed to the bed and the rumpled covers. A weakness attacked her legs, but she made them support her. What had begun as a blissful awakening had ended in such turmoil that she felt torn apart.

Pet released her tense frustration in a flurry of activity, going to the closet and dragging out her faded jeans. She grabbed a soft chamois blouse, as well, and tossed them both on the bed.

Chapter Eight

Pet dressed in a hurry, taking time only to put some lipstick on and tie a green scarf into a knot that gathered the hair at the nape of her neck. Leaving the room, she mentally braced herself for Lon's inquisition, but he wasn't in the lobby when she reached it.

Dane was, however, looking out a window in a relaxed stance. But when he turned to meet her, she realized he wasn't relaxed at all. He was a coiled spring, all poised to unleash that contained energy.

"Where's Lon?" Pet glanced around, knowing she wouldn't find him, but the action provided her with a few seconds to readjust her defenses.

The dark impatience of his eyes swept her. "I imagine he's at the center by now."

"He said he'd wait for me," she reminded him.

"I changed his mind." Dane stated what she had already guessed.

"I fully hope that you intend to give me a ride, otherwise I'll be without transportation to work." There was the right inflection of challenging humor in her cool voice to make it a casual remark. Her raw nerves hadn't betrayed her.

"I don't need to be reminded that you prefer work to a morning in bed with me. You've already made that clear." His smoothness was like the flat edge of a blade stroked threateningly across tender skin, and she paled a little at its silken quality of steel. "My car is out front."

"Shall we go?" Pet walked to the door without waiting for him.

Outside, she had to wait beside the sporty Jaguar while he unlocked it. Anger was in every controlled move he made, from the severely polite way he opened the car door for her to the deadly quiet way he shut it. Pet felt she was sitting on the edge of a volcano with an eruption minutes away, unsure whether the first blast would kill her or if she would be swept down the slopes on a river of molten lava. In any case, she doubted that she would come away unscathed.

An unearthly silence reigned until Dane turned the car onto the main road. "What was that idiotic remark about roses and mirrored ceilings all about?" He stabbed her with a glance, his features hard and uncompromising.

Pet continued to look straight ahead. "It should be self-explanatory," she shrugged.

"Then I must be incredibly dense, because I can't make head or tail of it," Dane replied in a tautly edged voice.

"I've heard that's a problem when you sleep in a round bed. It's impossible to tell the head of the bed from the foot." Pet forced the casual response.

A muscle played along the edge of his strong jaw. "I should have known this was all tied up with Ruby." He released a heavy breath that held anger and impatience. "You're jealous of her."

"You're mistaken," she denied calmly while a hot pain twisted her stomach. "I'm not interested in anything she has."

"And you think she has me?" he mocked, the corners of his mouth deepening in derision.

"Haven't you heard?" Pet cast him a false look of surprise. "It's common knowledge."

"And you believe it," Dane challenged with a hard glance.

"Do you deny it?" she countered.

"I didn't think I had to." On that half-savage note, he pressed his foot on the accelerator to send the Jaguar shooting past the slower car in front of them. It was an awesome display of power and agility that Pet found somehow characteristic of him.

"I'm sure you didn't. There are probably plenty of women who would be glad to go to bed with you without caring who else you might be sleeping with, but I'm not one of them," Pet stated when the burst of speed was over.

"And what was last night? A momentary lapse of moral principles?" Dane mocked derisively.

"I didn't go to bed with you." It was a moot point but the only defense she had.

"No, but you were damned well willing!" he reminded her brutally. "Or are you forgetting that you were undressing me!"

Her cheeks flamed with the memory of it. "I'm trying very hard to forget that."

But Dane didn't pay attention to her tightly worded reply. "In another fifteen minutes the boys would have walked in on something much more intimate than a simple embrace."

"That's something we'll never know, because they didn't walk in fifteen minutes later," she retorted, her hands clenched tightly in her lap.

"Are you going to deny —" he began angrily.

"Physically . . . sexually, you excite me, so I'm not going to deny your ability to make me feel aroused," she interrupted, since he wouldn't believe her if she tried. "But I don't wish to pursue an involvement with you. Their arrival was a mixed blessing. It saved me from making a stupid mistake."

There were two long beats of tense silence, then Dane prompted, "And? If it was a mixed blessing, there must be something you regret."

"There are two things. One, that it happened in the first place, and second, that they had to see me with you at all." She stared out the window, sitting rigidly in the seat. "I've worked so hard to get them to accept me as an equal. Now," she laughed bitterly, "I can just imagine what some of them are thinking. That I thought they weren't good enough, so I went after the boss."

Just as quickly as the bitter anger had surfaced, it vanished on a sigh. Pet brushed a limp hand over her face. "I should have had my head examined for going to that party with you last night. I was crazy to let myself in for all this grief."

"If you're so concerned about their opinion, you should have yelled 'Rape!' last night," he taunted.

"I wish I'd thought of it," she lied. "I would have."

When they reached the turn to the center, Dane took the corner fast, the low-slung sports car hugging the curb as it whipped around it with a squeal of tires. He braked abruptly near a side entrance where men were entering and exiting to get all the gear loaded.

As Pet reached for the door handle, Dane said, "You can tell the boys I'm docking your pay for being late this morning. I know you won't want them to think I'm showing you any favoritism." There was a sarcastic curve to his cruelly thin mouth.

"Thanks." She matched his tone as she climbed out of the car and slammed the door.

She had one foot on the curb when he leaned across the seat to add, "By the way, I haven't slept with Ruby since a green-eyed blonde invited me into her room to tuck her in. So you might give me credit for some degree of constancy," he accused harshly, and gunned the motor before accelerating away.

Momentarily stunned, Pet couldn't persuade her legs to move. She stared after the fast-moving car and its driver. What exactly had he said? She knew the words, but what did they mean? *No, no,* she admonished herself, *don't get your hopes up. Don't be a fool. You were right — it's just a physical thing, and the last complication you need in your life is an involvement with your boss.*

Heads turned when she entered the building. Self-conscious, she paused, aware of the hushing of voices. Squaring her shoulders, she walked briskly forward to the partially dismantled studio camera at the number-two position.

"We wondered if you were going to show up for work this morning." Charlie said what was on everyone's mind, but with a teasing gentleness.

"Why not?" Pet shrugged, and hopped onto the platform. "I'm a working girl."

"But what are you working at?" Lon taunted.

She guessed that his sarcasm came from bitter resentment and jealousy that Dane had succeeded where he had failed. She understood the fragility of his male ego, but that didn't prevent her from defending herself.

"I know how it looked last night." There was a hint of pink in her cheeks, but she didn't hang her head. "I don't blame any of you for what you thought. I'm just as susceptible to a good line as the next person. You're going to believe what you want to regardless of what I say, so let's just drop the subject."

"Pet's right," Andy agreed. "We've got a lot of work to do."

By the middle of the afternoon all the equipment had been packed and loaded up, and after a stop at the hotel to pick up their luggage, the production crew went out for the next location. The majority of the technicians and equipment would head for Atlantic City. Pet was among the group destined for Batsto; the outdoor segments were to be taped there.

Riding in the passenger seat of Charlie's snubnosed van, Pet incuriously watched the Sunday traffic on the Garden State Parkway. Rick Benton, one of the sound men, and Ted, a lighting technician, were sitting on the black fur cot at the back, part of the skeleton crew that would be needed.

"Don't forget to watch for my exit," Charlie reminded her, not for the first time. "We'll probably get lost before we get there."

"I doubt it," Pet offered dryly.

"I'd like to know whose harebrained idea this was," he muttered. "Location shots in New Jersey of all places!"

"New Jersey is more than a corridor you have to pass through between New York and Pennsylvania." Her state pride insisted that she couldn't let that remark go unchallenged. "I know that's all most people see as they zoom through on their way someplace else. No one wants to believe we have swamp, marshes, miles of beach, farms, forests and lakes. If they can't see it from the highway, it isn't there."

"This must have been your idea, then," Charlie declared with a laughing glance.

"Why do you think it's called the Garden State?" she retorted, ignoring his remark.

"Because it has 'gardens' of concrete," he joked. "That's all I've ever seen. Hey!" He smiled broadly. "I just thought of something. Ruby Gale is the lily of the Garden State. That's a pretty good slogan, isn't it? Why don't you mention that to Dane?"

"Why me?" Pet stiffened because she knew precisely why. Charlie believed she was on very friendly terms with Dane. She could have been, but she wasn't going to go into a long, detailed explanation of why she wasn't anymore. "It was your idea. You tell him."

"He'd be more apt to listen to you, wouldn't he?" Charlie probed for information.

"I seriously doubt it," she replied with assumed indifference.

At that moment a midnight-blue Jaguar swept past them. Her heart did a somersault at the sight of the familiar car. It was highly unlikely that there would be two identical cars on the road. When she saw Ruby Gale's red head in the passenger seat, she knew she hadn't made a mistake about the car's owner.

"That was Ruby Gale, wasn't it?" Charlie frowned.

"Yes, with Dane," she added briskly, and sent him a cool look. "Do you still think he would listen to me?"

Charlie took one look at her strained face and let the conversation die a natural death. Confusion tore at Pet. Dane had indicated that his interest in Ruby Gale had waned since meeting her. But Ruby had been riding with him. Was it because of the television special — purely business? Or, because Pet herself had turned him down, had Dane turned to Ruby again?

Why were the answers so important? Her heart was becoming involved, that was why, a little voice warned. Pet sighed dejectedly and gazed out the window. The Jaguar was far out of sight.

Located on the fringes of Wharton State Forest, Batsto Village was a restored Revolutionary War town. Growing up around an early bog-iron furnace, it was a major supplier of munitions to the colonists. There were tours of old houses, coach rides and demonstrations of an operating water-powered sawmill. Weekend fare also included craft displays and flea markets. The picturesque colonial town sat on the bank of the Batsto River with shaded streets and the verdant backdrop of the forest.

There was no work to be done on their arrival. All the location shots would be set up the following morning, which left Pet and the small crew free to wander through the village on the late and lazy summer afternoon.

Pet would have been content to stroll along the streets and browse through the curio tables, but typically the men were soon bored with such passive entertainment. Someone produced a Frisbee, and before Pet knew what was happening she was engaged in a lively game of catch in a park square. It was boisterous fun, leaping high to catch the soaring disk and trying difficult catches behind the back or under the leg. It was exactly the kind of distraction her tense nerves needed.

The Frisbee came sailing in her direction, but just as she got set to catch it, the wind caught it to change its trajectory. The disk drifted backward, and Pet realized at the last minute that it was going to be high and to her right. She turned to make a diving leap for it and rammed right into a solid object.

Her not inconsiderable height and weight staggered Dane backward, but she managed to keep them both upright. Pet wasn't sure if it was the impact or the shock of finding herself in his arms that stole the breath from her lungs. She stayed there, unable to breathe for several seconds while her fingers were spread across his chest and her head was thrown back as she stared into his vitally male face.

Her hair had long ago escaped the confining knot of the scarf and was a windblown mass of wheat gold. Dane's hands were on her waist, holding her hips against the disturbing support of his thighs. Desire flamed rawly through her when his gaze drifted down to linger on her mouth.

Her lips parted, wanting his kiss, inviting it, and there was an answering tightness in the grip of his hands to let her know the message had been received and understood. There was even a faint movement of his dark head in her direction.

"You really should watch where you're going," a musically female voice chided.

Pet's startled green eyes clashed with a pair of vivid blue ones that studied her with a calculating coldness. The sight of Ruby Gale standing near Dane brought her quickly to her senses. She pushed out of his hold, nervously brushing her palms over the terry-cloth material of her shorts, the blue jeans abandoned earlier in the day in favor of something cooler.

"Excuse me," she apologized to Dane on a breathless note.

"No harm done," he assured her as a mocking grimness tautened his expression.

"Hey, Pet! Are you going to get the Frisbee or not?" Charlie shouted from across the way.

Glancing around, Pet saw that it had landed a few feet behind Dane. Before she could retrieve it, Dane was there bending over to pick it up. His gaze raked her as he straightened. She was conscious of the perspiration shining wetly on the skin of her neck, beads gathering in the hollows of her collar bone to start a trickle running down between her breasts. The thin cotton knit of her tank top was clinging to her damp skin. Dane made her aware of just how revealing it was before he returned the Frisbee.

"Thank you," she murmured awkwardly, and turned away. He couldn't know how much he had contributed to the color in her hotly flushed cheeks.

Taking a few quick steps, she sailed the Frisbee back to Charlie with a flick of her wrist. But it took a nose dive short of its target, and a shirtless Charlie came trotting forward to retrieve it.

"You're welcome to join us if you like, Miss Gale," Charlie invited, puffing slightly behind his wide grin.

"No, thank you." The redhead refused with a laughing recoil at the thought. She sent a coy glance at Dane and slipped a hand under his arm. "Dane would hate it if I looked as hot and disheveled as she does," she declared with a pointed glance at Pet.

Pet had been conscious of her appearance before, but that remark made her doubly uncomfortable. Which was just what the star wanted. Ruby looked as if she had just stepped out of an advertisement for sports clothes in her snow-white skirt and candy-pink blouse.

Rather than stay where the contrast in their appearance was so marked, Pet decided to switch with one of the others. "Let me have the shady side for a while, Rick." If she looked hot and disheveled, there wasn't any point in quitting. Besides, she didn't want to give Ruby Gale the satisfaction of knowing she made her feel self-conscious and unattractive.

After she had traded places with the sound man, she saw Dane and Ruby strolling away arm in arm. It hurt, because she wanted to be the one walking with Dane. If she had stayed in bed, it was entirely possible she could have been. She shook her head to rid it of that tantalizing thought.

Monday morning meant a return to the work schedule, rising early to get the equipment ready and the outdoor shots set up. The weather cooperated with a clear sunny day, a warm temperature and little breeze to mess the star's coiffure.

There was no need for headsets or lights. The smaller and lighter-weight hand-held camera took the place of the fixed studio models, although it meant a helper was needed to carry the recorder. Someone was walking through Ruby's positions so it could be decided where the shiny reflectors would be needed to alleviate facial shadows.

Dane had already explained the setup to Pet in crisp, strictly businesslike tones. She was strapping on the battery packs that powered the camera and the shoulder pad to cushion its weight. The equipment had all been tested to make sure it was working properly. Now they were waiting for Ruby Gale to emerge from her private motor home/dressing room. Pet cast another glance in its direction, acutely aware that Dane was with the red-haired entertainer.

When they came out together, she quickly veiled her glance. But she noticed his arm affectionately around the woman's shoulders, the warmth and charm in his look, and the easy way he responded to Ruby's provocative glances. He was going over the particular sequence of this taping and reiterating the effect he planned to achieve.

Pet hoisted the camera onto her shoulder and adjusted it to a relatively comfortable position. While Dane walked Ruby to her starting point, Pet began lining up her opening frame. Her long hair was swept on top of her head, secured on the sides with combs and on top with a leather hair poke. With it loose there was too much risk of catching a strand on a part of the camera or between the pad and her shoulder, which often resulted in a sudden and painful yank on her scalp when she moved or altered position.

Dane's gaze made an absent inspection of her hairstyle as he approached her, but it was the only recognition of her sex that he made. His rugged features were impassive, all his attention focused on the business at hand. The fluttering of her pulse revealed that she had not achieved his objectivity.

"Ready, Wallis?" His gaze centered on her for a piercing second, long enough to see her positive nod. When he turned away, virile charm leaped from the smile he gave Ruby. "We can begin whenever you say, Ruby."

If he had wanted to make clear the difference in his attitude toward the two women, he had succeeded. Pet felt almost chilled by his callous lack of interest. Instead of being enchanted by the warmth Dane had shown the star, Ruby Gale appeared anything but pleased.

"What's *she* doing here?" she demanded, and pointed a scarlet fingernail at Pet.

"She's operating the camera, of course," Dane smiled.

"How can I possibly flirt with the camera the way you want when I'm looking at her?" Ruby protested with an angry gesture of her hands.

"Flirt with the lens, my love, and think of the male audience that will ultimately be watching you," he replied easily, using that smile again.

But Ruby wasn't to be persuaded. "That's impossible! I want a man on that camera. Get rid of her!" She flung an impatient hand in Pet's direction. "I want her off the set."

"Darling, you aren't being reasonable." Dane moved toward the star.

"Do you want to know how unreasonable I can be?" the redhead flashed, exhibiting the temper Pet had heard so much about. "Either she goes or I do. Take your pick, Dane. You can't have us both."

There was silence all around. The ultimatum seemed to have a dual meaning. Pet was well aware which one would go even before she heard the low chuckle from Dane.

"Darling, I'm not arguing with you," he insisted calmly, amused by her outburst. "There isn't any need to make an issue of it. If you're more comfortable with someone else operating the camera, then I'll simply replace Miss Wallis. As lovely as you are when you're angry, I would rather you conserved all that volatile energy for your performance."

Ruby Gale was instantly and provocatively contrite. "Darling, I'm sorry for making a horrible scene. Will you forgive me?"

"Naturally I forgive you." He bent to brush a kiss across her cheek and turned to dismiss Pet. "Sutton will handle the camera today, Miss Wallis. We won't need you."

"Certainly." Her voice was barely above a whisper as she acknowledged his order.

As she shifted the camera off her shoulder to set it on the ground, Charlie moved over to help her. His eyebrows were raised in a sympathetic look. She managed a grim smile and a supposedly uncaring shrug, then began unstrapping the bulky packs from around her waist.

"It will take us a few minutes, I'm afraid, to switch the equipment," Dane explained to Ruby. "Why don't you relax and have another cup of coffee while you're waiting? There's no need for you to stand around."

"Are you sure you don't mind, Dane, about

using a cameraman?" the redhead persisted. "I'd hate to think I was interfering in your job."

"If I thought she was irreplacable, I would argue with you. So you needn't be concerned that you've upset me," he assured her.

As soon as Pet had removed all the gear and given it to Charlie, she slipped self-consciously away from the location set. She was aware that Dane had observed her departure without comment. By getting rid of her, he had averted a scene and a possible delay. It had been the sensible thing to do, she knew that, but it did sting to be rejected so readily.

Chapter Nine

Sitting beneath the shade of a tree with the trunk for a backrest, Pet laid the paperback book aside. It couldn't hold her interest, or else she wasn't concentrating. She sighed and plucked a long blade of grass to twirl it between her fingers. Eyeing the sun, she wondered if its lengthening shadows had called a halt to the day's shooting yet. In a little while she would wander over to Charlie's van and wait, but it was cooler here and more peaceful, although her surroundings didn't seem to soothe her.

A bird flitted in the branches overhead. Drawing her knees up, she pulled the blade of grass apart and discarded the pieces. It was worse having nothing to do. Finally she pushed to her feet and absently dusted the seat of her pants. The soft rustle of footsteps on the grass turned her head toward the sound.

A breath stopped in her throat. Dane was walking toward her, lithe and supple. His gaze never ceased its study of her while he approached, gauging her reaction to his arrival. Pet knew her eyes could be much too expressive, so she made a casual half turn, bending to pick up her book.

"Are you finished for the day?" She was able

to ask the question without having to look at him.

"We wrapped it up about twenty minutes ago. Too many shadows." He leaned a hand on the rough bark of the tree trunk and let his gaze roam the surroundings. "It's peaceful here."

"Yes," she agreed. Her glance slid away before it actually met his. "Charlie will be waiting for me, then."

"He was packing the equipment up when I left. I told him I'd find you and send you along to his van." Dane continued to study her with disconcerting directness.

"He'd probably like some help. I'd better go." But she didn't want to leave.

"Pet, about this morning, it wasn't by choice that I ordered you off the set." His dark eyes were grave as they searched her face, waiting for her response.

"I know." She looked across the green grass to the village center, liking its quaintness. "You did it because you had to keep Ruby happy for the sake of the production."

"Yes." He reached out to take hold of her forearm and force her to look at him. "But who's going to keep *me* happy? Will you?"

Unable to answer, Pet could only gaze into the masculine face with its tanned skin drawn tight over angular features. But the longing to be the one who could keep him happy was written in her jade eyes. She heard his sharply indrawn breath, then his

166

mouth was coming down to crush hers.

His arm hooked her waist to haul her against his length. The contact with the taut columns of his thighs and hard flatness of his stomach made her weak. Her hands clutched his waist, hanging on while the world spinned at a dizzying speed. Nothing seemed to exist as her mouth opened under his passionately to return the hungry kiss. Then his hand moved onto her breast, circling it, cupping it, flattening it, and fighting the restriction of her blouse. When she felt his fingers tugging at the buttons, she partially returned to her senses and pulled breathlessly away, half pivoting out of his arms while she had the strength.

"Don't!" There was a catch in her voice, a deep, tearing desire interfering with the protest.

"Don't what?" Dane yanked her around, punishing her with his hard grip while his angry gaze burned her already heated flesh. "Don't touch you! Don't hold you! Don't kiss you! Don't what? Don't want you? That's impossible!" he raged in a savagely low voice. "I've tried. I've tried it all — working till all hours of the night, cold showers, and endless recriminations for getting mixed up with someone who works for me! It hasn't changed a damned thing."

Pet was shaken by the ferocity of his emotional response. This intensity was more than she had bargained for. She didn't know how to cope with it, any more than she knew how to

167

handle her own abandonment of common sense.

When he slackened his hold, she didn't try to escape him. There was no resistance as his hands moved to her hair to release it from the confinement of the combs and leather poke. His fingers slipped through its length and gathered it into silken handfuls.

"You have beautiful hair, Pet," he groaned, and rubbed his mouth across her cheekbone, drawing closer to her lips. His breath was warm and moist, caressing on its own. "I keep seeing it this way — the way it was yesterday morning, a tawny, rumpled cloud on your pillow. I never should have used that key, or else I should have thrown Baxter out."

"Why didn't you tell me you weren't . . . involved with Ruby anymore?" Her voice throbbed as her arms curved around his middle.

"Why didn't you ask me?" Dane countered. "God, I thought I'd made it obvious. Do you actually believe I would invite another woman to a party given by my mistress if she and I were still lovers?"

"You . . . you could have been having your cake and eating it, too." Pet recalled the phrase the reporter had used. It had sounded so plausible at the time.

"I could have." He tugged at a handful of hair to force her head back. His gaze seemed to stab deeply into her. "But I'm not the type.

What are you doubting now? I can see it in your eyes. Very expressive eyes they are, too."

"I was just wondering how you knew about the rose canopy above her bed," Pet admitted, because the question would plague her until she knew. "You said you hadn't slept with her lately, but —"

"I haven't." Irritation put a harsh edge on his voice. "All entertainers seem to have little eccentricities; hers happens to be going over new arrangements while sitting in bed. In order to have a discussion of them, it seems logical to join her on the bed. I suppose I could have pulled a chair up, but I don't happen to be bashful or easily embarrassed."

"But you and she were lovers."

"Yes, we were lovers, for the lack of a better term." The flaring of his nostrils revealed his dislike of Pet's continued pursuit of the subject. "Do you expect me to be a virgin?"

Pet attempted a negative shake of her head, and succeeded as much as his grip on her hair would allow. "I just wondered if you were always so quick to discard a woman once you grew tired of her." Because she wasn't certain how well she would take it if he dropped her as quickly as he had seemed to abandon Ruby Gale. "Everyone still believes the two of you are having an affair," she reminded him when she saw the darkening anger in his eyes. "You act like it when you're together."

"As you pointed out earlier, I have to keep

her happy. Dammit, Pet," he muttered in exasperation, "you know how costly delays can be. No other producer would touch Ruby with a ten-foot pole. Her reputation for walking off a production or causing endless changes has thrown a hundred budgets out the window. A television special with her can be a gold mine if it doesn't cost you two gold mines to get it. I'm walking a tightrope with her. Why do you think I'm personally handling this project?"

"How far would you go to keep her happy, Dane?" Pet hated herself for asking, because it wasn't fair. She had no right to ask that kind of question.

"You have to ask!" He stared at her, an incredulous frown narrowing his gaze.

"Dane, I'm not sure about anything," Pet whispered on a tiny sob. "I'm unsure of how I feel, what I think, what I do. Every ounce of sense I have tells me I shouldn't want you, but I do."

With a muffled groan he pulled her forward against the hard warmth of his mouth. The hand at the nape of her neck began stroking it softly and sensuously, sending shivers tingling down her spine. A faint hungry sound rolled from her throat as she arched against him, surrendering to this wild joy that flamed from his kiss.

When she wound her arms around his neck, his mouth parted in an irresistible invitation to deepen the kiss, and Pet accepted it eagerly. In direct response, his hand flattened convulsively on her hips, shaping her more firmly to him to give her potent evidence of his need, and she trembled uncontrollably.

Abruptly Dane dragged his mouth from hers, the hand at the back of her head applying pressure to bury her face against his neck while shudders racked his torso. She could feel the hard, uneven thud of his heart. The rate of her own pulse would have rivaled the speed of his car. Happiness was such a fragile thing. Its beauty filled her eyes with tears and swelled her heart to the point of bursting. How could she ever contemplate denying this ecstasy that she was a kiss away from discovering?

Her hands spread across the broad muscularity of his back to hold him closer while her lips began exploring his throat, savoring the taste of his skin and absorbing the heat of his flesh. In a slow, roundabout way she reached his ear, her tongue delighting in the shape of it. A raw sound of desire came from his throat before he turned his head to stop the arousing caress, his mouth rough against her cheek and his breathing heavy.

"Don't," he ordered in a low, thickened voice.

"Don't what?" she whispered, and teased him with his words while her fingertips sensuously traced the strong column of his neck. "Don't want you. Don't kiss you. Don't —"

Angrily he silenced her with a hard, bruising

kiss that was brief in its fury. Then he growled against her skin, "Half the time I never know whether to kill you or kiss you!"

"I prefer the latter," Pet murmured, careless of the provocation in her reply. The world had stopped its frenzied spinning, but she wasn't ready to get off.

His hands firmly created a space between them, the support of his hard length denied her as he held her a few inches away. Her gaze ran warmly over the rough planes of his essentially male features, aware of the sobered slash of his mouth.

"We've got to come to an understanding," he insisted. "These next few days aren't going to be easy." In a trembling underbreath he reluctantly issued, "God, that's an understatement!" Then he turned his hard gaze away from her for an instant.

"I think you could be right," Pet sighed, because it was hard staying out of his arms. It was always like that when she was near him.

"I know I am. Pet —" he used her name so he could have her complete attention, which had become distracted by the opened neckline of his shirt and the springy chest hairs it revealed "— I have to leave now for Atlantic City. There are a few details I have to iron out with the management at the casino. Then I have to be back here for the taping tomorrow. We aren't going to have any time to be together."

"I see." She didn't ask if she could go with

him. If Dane had wanted her along, he would have invited her. He had to know she would accept.

"I still have a company to run, so my schedule is going to be like this until this damned special is done," he said, revealing his impatience and irritation at the circumstances, which offered some consolation. "I want you to understand that isn't the way I want it. I don't want you getting any crazy notions in your head that because I'm not with you, I don't want to be. No more of that imagination of yours working overtime about rose canopies and being patronized or whatever ridiculous molehill you can make into a mountain."

"No more." Pet shook her head in promise.

"There's another thing you'd better know. I don't give a damn what the crew thinks about us. You can keep on trying to be one of the boys if you want. But if I get a chance to touch you or kiss you, don't you dare shy away from me because one of them might be watching," Dane warned. "I'll be discreet. There won't be any passionate clinches in front of them, but I'm not going to guard my every look and action. If they want to accuse you of receiving special treatment, you can tell them for me that you damned well *are* special! Any objections?"

"None. Half of them think we've already slept together anyway," she admitted, a little thrilled by his possessiveness.

"I wish we had. Maybe I wouldn't be twisted

into so many hard knots inside." His gaze raked her, smoldering with the frustration of unsatisfied desire. Pet saw the effort he made to get a grip on himself, to bank the fires that burned in his eyes. "There's still the matter of Ruby to be settled," he added.

"Dane, I —" Pet began.

"Listen to me," he insisted. "She has to be the center of attention all the time. She won't share the spotlight with anyone. So when I'm around her, it will appear that I'm totally indifferent to you. You saw what happened this morning the second she suspected my interests weren't wholly devoted to her. She immediately made a scene. It doesn't matter to Ruby whether the attention she receives is genuine or not, just so long as she can command it. Until this taping is wrapped up, she will *appear* to have my undivided attention. Do you accept that?"

"Yes," she nodded, beginning to understand the spoiled and self-centered temperament of the talented performer. It also explained why Dane had been so very attentive to the star.

"You know she isn't going to let you work on the taping tomorrow." Dane eyed her with grim resignation. "She's going to keep you off the studio cameras at the casino, too, which means you'll be working the hand-held, providing she doesn't demand that you leave the production altogether."

"Maybe it would be best if I did. I don't want

to cause problems. You can get someone to replace me," she suggested. "I can go back —"

"No." He rejected that idea out of hand. "You aren't going back, not even if I have to replace you. You're going to stay with the crew. You aren't going back until we all go home. I know I'll be working all the time and maybe I'll only get to see you five — ten minutes, half an hour at a time. But I'll know you're there and if I get the chance to be with you, I will."

Keeping her at a distance, he kissed her, his mouth clinging to her lips for an enchanting instant before he lifted his head. The sweet torment of longing made his expression bleak and grim. Pet wanted to smooth away the hardness in his face with her hand, but he wouldn't let her touch him, as if not trusting his reaction.

"You said before that you were unsure," Dane said tightly. "Maybe you can appreciate the way I feel. The times I've been with you haven't been among my more rational moments. It's like being trapped between two battling weather fronts — one hot and the other cold. I never know which it's going to be with you."

"You pick a lot of the fights yourself." Pet wasn't that submissive that she would accept full responsibility for their arguments. He had been at fault, too. "You shouldn't say things you know will irritate me."

"Maybe I have." He granted that it was possible without admitting it. "From now on, un-

175

derstand the pressure I'm under. If I'm sharp with you, be tolerant . . . at least until this taping is done. I'd sell my soul to have it finished right now." Then Dane laughed, a wry sound. "Some say I made a pact with the devil when I signed the contract with Ruby."

"Don't laugh!" A sudden pain brought a quick frown to her forehead. "It isn't funny."

Dane stared at her, his eyes narrowing in anger. "I don't want to know what you're thinking right now. I haven't got time to correct whatever erroneous impression is forming in that mind of yours." He raised an arm to glance at his watch. "I'm already five minutes late. Ruby will be wondering where I am."

"Ruby?" Pet stiffened. "I thought you said you were driving to Atlantic City?"

"I am," he said tightly, and released her.

"She's going with you." Her voice sounded remarkably flat.

"Yes, she's going with me. She wants to check on the dressing rooms backstage. God help us if they aren't up to her standards," Dane grumbled, and irritatedly ran a hand over his hair.

"I'm sure you'll make it right, Dane." Pet managed a smile, an attempt at reassurance, yet strangely the words had an ominous ring to them.

"I have to go," he said as if needing to impress her with the inevitability of it.

"I know. Go ahead." This time she really

worked at the smile and it felt more natural. "Tell Charlie I'll be along in a minute. I just have to gather up my things." Such as the combs and the hair poke he had scattered on the ground, as well as her handbag and the book she'd been trying to read.

Dane took a step away. "I probably won't see you until tomorrow."

"Drive carefully." A sarcastic little voice wanted to add, *the star of the show will be riding with you and nothing must happen to her.* But Pet didn't let that voice speak.

Although Pet wasn't present during the next morning's taping, she gathered from what Charlie had intimated at lunch that it wasn't going well. Ruby Gale was being difficult and demanding, and Dane wasn't satisfied with the results they were getting. Only the crew knew of his displeasure, from what Pet could tell. Not a shadow of blame was ever cast on the star.

Professional curiosity got the better of her. Bored, with nothing else to do, she wandered over to the mobile television unit parked some distance from the shooting site. The snub-nosed van was no bigger than Charlie's. She tried the door and found it was unlocked. Even though the van was parked in the shade, it was stuffy and hot inside. She left the sliding door open to let the fresh air in.

The interior was equipped with a monitor and

a videotape player among other things. Those were the two items that interested Pet, along with the three-quarter-inch cassettes she found on top of the player. Charlie's handwriting on the labels identified the contents as part of this location's taping. She punched them into the player and adjusted the monitor screen, sitting back on the little stool to see what had been taped and what might be wrong with it.

Twice she played them through, nagged by something she knew wasn't right yet unable to fault the performer or the cameraman. The lighting was perfect and so was the background. Punching the cassettes in for the third time, she kept asking herself how they could be improved.

Halfway through it the third time, Pet had the germ of an idea. She stopped the tape, rewound it and punched it through again. In her mind she made the changes, the additions, and checked them mentally to see if they would work. The elation grew with each passing second.

"No one's allowed in there!" Dane snapped the order before he saw it was Pet inside the van. "What are you doing?"

"I know what's wrong!" She stopped the tape and pushed the rewind button.

"You know what's wrong, do you?" he mocked. "What's wrong is you haven't kissed me hello."

"I was talking about the tape." But she

quickly brushed her lips across his mouth and grabbed hold of the hand that reached out for her. She pulled him inside, too excited by her discovery to be put off by his impatient look.

"What about the taping? There aren't any problems," he denied as he crouched to keep from bumping his head on the van's ceiling.

"Charlie mentioned at lunch that you weren't pleased with what you had, but you couldn't find anything wrong with it. I got curious and since I didn't have anything to do anyway —"

"You decided to snoop," he concluded.

"It isn't snooping," she protested. "I work on the production, too. There's nothing wrong with wanting to see the results." She was kneeling in front of the tape player, anxiously waiting for it to finish rewinding.

"I've looked at those tapes fifty times. I'm taking what we've got, Pet. Let's not waste time looking at them again." Dane slid his hand across her stomach to hook her waist and attempt to draw her back to where he was sitting on the stool.

She pushed his hand away. "But I know how you can improve it." The tape had finally stopped rewinding and she could punch it up on the monitor.

"I happen to be an experienced director. Are you trying to tell me how to do my job?" There was a thin thread of anger in his incredulous question.

"Be quiet and throw your manly pride away."

Pet flashed him an irritated glance. "You could listen and give me a chance to explain my idea."

"I'll listen." He sat back on the stool, folding his arms in front of him and looking anything but open-minded.

"You could give me credit for knowing a little about what I'm talking about, instead of acting so damned superior," she retorted.

His mouth twitched. "Didn't I tell you once how to shut me up if I was making you angry?"

"The problem is that you've made me too angry to do it. If I kissed you, you'd like it, then it wouldn't be a punishment," Pet reasoned in a thinly impatient tone.

Pivoting on her knees, she turned to watch the screen, which put her back to Dane. His hands closed firmly on her shoulders to draw her back to rest against his legs. Lifting the weight of her hair, he gently draped it over her shoulder.

"Then sit next to me, because that will definitely be a torment," he gently mocked. When she turned her head to look up at him, regret for her sharpness flashing in her green eyes, his finger pushed her chin toward the screen. "Show me what you found."

"You were experimenting with camera angles," she began as the first take was being played, minus the sound since it wasn't a problem. "But it's the elevation that's wrong."

"The elevation?" By his tone she could tell

that this hadn't occurred to him and his mind was racing in examination of the tape the same way hers had.

"Yes. Charlie should be up high and shooting down; up about five feet, I would say. Maybe smear some Vaseline around the circumference of the lens so the outer edges of the picture will be in a kind of dreamy focus. And here —" she drew attention to the particular sequence "— where Ruby does that half turn to the right, Charlie should make a half turn to the left — sort of a sweeping arc with the camera to give that illusion," she explained with growing enthusiasm. "It will be tricky. Some sort of ladder or scaffolding."

"I wonder where I can get a crane," Dane mused.

"It's obvious that would be best, but there's the time factor, and the delay it means. I think you can rig something up — Charlie's good at that kind of thing. And here —" another part came up that she had an idea for "— the camera could swing a little bit in tempo with the music."

Turning, she found Dane was leaning forward to watch another take, visualizing her ideas in place of the ones that had been used. His expression was a study of concentration and inward reflection. She nibbled at her lip, anxious for his reaction and certain it had to be positive.

But there was only silence that lasted through

two more takes. Unable to wait any longer, Pet unconsciously swayed against him and laid a hand on his thigh, her fingers curling into the hard flesh. She was immediately the recipient of his glance.

"What do you think?" she asked.

"I think you pick the damnedest times to touch me." His eyes glinted with a wicked, dancing light before directing a glance out the open door to a crew member approaching the van. "And I think you do it deliberately." His hand closed warmly over hers and moved it to a more discreet location near his knee.

A hot wave of color flooded her cheeks, but he wouldn't let her look away from him, holding her gaze with some invisible thread. Pet was jolted by the intimacy of the moment — an intimacy that didn't rely on a kiss or a caress, but could be accomplished with a look.

"In answer to your question, you've come up with the solution," Dane admitted. "I doubt if we can achieve that pirouette shot unless Charlie is directly above her."

"We're all set up for the next number, Mr. Kingston," Rick announced, pausing at the open door of the van. "Are you coming? I'll bring the new tape Charlie wanted."

"I'll be there in a minute." He opened the storage cabinet to take out a clean cassette tape. "Here." He tossed it to the man, then began uncoiling his length to maneuver himself out of the cramped quarters of the van.

Pet followed him out, hopping the last foot to the ground, a hand on the door frame for balance. "Do you admit that I did know what I was talking about?" she asked in half challenge, her green eyes sparkling at his previous arrogant skepticism.

Dane paused, running his eyes over her in dry amusement. "I admit it. Now why don't you suggest how I'm going to convince Miss Gale to do that number again without arousing her temper?"

"Keeping her happy is strictly your department," she retorted, conscious that Rick was dawdling on his way back to the location, remaining within sight of them.

Dane was aware of him, too. His hand stroked her hair, then traced the clean line of her jaw to her chin, where his fingers outlined her lips. The sensual caress started her trembling.

"Aren't you sorry you didn't kiss me when you had the chance?" He tapped the end of her nose with a finger, an affectionate reprimand for her stubbornness. Without waiting for a reply, he walked after Rick.

Pet sighed.

Chapter Ten

Atlantic City is famous for its beach and the magic of its street names — Boardwalk, Ventnor Avenue, Baltic and Oriental Avenue — familiar to every child who has played the game of Monopoly, its creator having taken the names from this city's streets. The Miss America Beauty Pageant is held at Convention Hall on the Boardwalk, which now boasts gambling casinos.

The whirring reels and clanging bells of the slot machines dominated everything. At the tables, the voices of the gamblers and dealers seemed almost muted in comparison to the din of the machines. Pet followed Charlie as he elbowed his way through the crowd of guests eager to part with their money. Coins clattered into a metal tray and a woman shouted excitedly to her husband.

"It's really something, isn't it?" Charlie shook his head.

Pet laughed at his seeming disdain. "Five minutes after you put your things in your room, you'll be down here and you know it!"

He grinned suddenly and let his hand find her elbow where the crowd thinned, enabling them to walk together. "Don't tell Sandy. She'll have my hide," he said, referring to his wife.

"I won't," she promised.

"I'm hoping she'll be so glad to see me that she won't even know I'm a few dollars broker than when I left." He pushed the "up" arrow on the elevator. "I need some relaxation after these last three days. I thought Ruby was going to bring down the whole town with that screaming fit she threw when Dane told her we were going to reshoot that first segment. It was a great idea you had, Pet. It worked like a charm once Kingston talked her into it."

"I saw the tapes. It did look great," she agreed, but didn't comment on the star's out-rage over being asked to do the number again. Nor did she want to know too much about Dane's role in changing Ruby's mind.

"What are you going to do after you get your things in your room?" Charlie stepped aside when the elevator doors opened, and let Pet walk in ahead of him.

"Shower, then probably grab a sandwich." She supposed Dane would be busy that eve-ning. She had seen practically nothing of him the past two days.

"I'm hungry, too. We could eat together, if you want. It would keep my money in my pockets a little while longer," he grinned, and pushed the floor number for his room. "What floor for you?"

"The next one." One floor above him — Dane's travel arrangements again separated her from the male members of the crew.

"The place was probably too crowded for all of us to be together," Charlie offered his own explanation. "I'm surprised we're even booked into the same hotel as the casino."

"Dane probably didn't want to provide us with any excuses for being late," she shrugged.

"About the sandwich?"

"Sure, we can eat together." It was better than eating alone. "Where do you want to meet?"

The elevator stopped at his floor. "Why don't I just stop by your room in half an hour?" he suggested. "It will be easier than trying to find each other in that madhouse downstairs."

"Okay, but make it forty-five minutes. I want to wash my hair," Pet explained hurriedly, and he waved an acknowledgement before the elevator doors closed.

At the next floor Pet got off the elevator and found her room. She heard a phone ringing as she set her weekender bag down to unlock the door. Hurriedly Pet opened it, certain that the caller was Dane but the phone was silent when she stepped into the room. She wasn't even sure if it had been her phone that was ringing.

Opening her suitcase, she shook out the uncrushable dress she had brought with her, the only one, and laid it on the bed. The taupe and beige dress was simple almost to the point of plainness, with buttontab roll-up sleeves, deep side pockets and a tie belt. After more than a week of slacks and jeans, it would be a pleasant change to wear a dress, Pet decided.

She unpacked her makeup and shampoo from her cosmetic case and carried them into the bathroom. Forty-five minutes wasn't much time to shower, dry her hair and dress, so she left the rest of her things to unpack later, stripped and stepped into the shower.

Her hair was lathered with shampoo when she realized the phone was ringing, the sound muffled by the running water of the shower. Grabbing a towel, she made a quick dash for the phone in the bedroom, leaving a trail of water and shampoo bubbles on the carpet. It stopped ringing as she reached it. She waited a few dripping seconds before returning to the shower to rinse her hair.

It happened again when she was drying her hair with the blow dryer, the hum of the dryer blocking out the ring of the phone. Again the caller hung up before Pet reached the phone. If it was Dane, she was becoming thoroughly frustrated. She returned to the bathroom and finished drying her hair, shutting the motor off every few minutes to listen for the phone. Only it didn't ring.

Not until she was brushing her teeth. With a mouthful of toothpaste she ran into the bedroom and stubbed her toe on the end of the bed. An involuntary cry came from her throat at the shafts of pain that stabbed her injured toe. She hopped the last six steps to the phone. This time she heard the line click dead before she could get the receiver to her ear.

"Damn you, Dane Kingston," she cursed tearfully, then noticed the clock. It could have been Charlie, checking to see if she was ready early, she realized.

The thought lent impetus to her haste to dress. Five minutes before she was supposed to be ready, she buckled the strap of her beige sandals and reached for the tie belt to knot it around her waist. At the knock on her door, she glanced at the phone. She would positively scream if Dane called her after she had gone. But how would she know if she wasn't there?

The knock sounded more impatient. Sighing, she walked to the door while making the first loop in the knot of her belt. She was adjusting the trailing ends to hang smoothly down her side as she opened the door.

"Where the hell have you been?" Dane demanded, striding inside the room and slamming the door shut. "I've been trying to reach you for the last forty-five minutes!" Pet's surprise turned to indignant shock at his raging demands that didn't permit her a reply. "I've called three times without an answer. The desk verified that you checked in more than a half hour ago. I finally called Charlie to find out where the hell you were and he told me you were on your way up here when he left you. I've been half out of my mind! Why didn't you answer the phone?"

"Why didn't you let the damned thing ring

long enough to give me a chance?" she hurled back at him with equal anger. "The first time I was just walking into the room. Then I was in the shower. And then I stubbed my toe trying to get in here because I knew it was you! How dare you yell at me, you arrogant, pigheaded —"

"No." The one low word cut across her angry retort, his hard features unrelenting in their severity. "We aren't going to have another shouting match, not this time! I've waited too long."

Seizing her shoulders, he jerked her against his lean, hard length. Pet struggled, resisting the appeasement of his bruising mouth, but she couldn't escape it. Twisting angrily within the steel circle of his arms, she beat at him with tight fists.

The sheer absurdity of her actions finally struck her, holding her motionless for an instant. This was what she wanted, where she wanted to be. Her arms went around his neck, her body becoming pliant to his hands.

The kiss that had been subjugating became deeply sensuous, and Pet returned it with equal passion, arching closer to him under the guidance of his shaping hands. His roaming caress excited her flesh, swamping her with the totality of her love, the sheer, sweet impossiblity of it.

When breathing was permitted again, she whispered achingly, "I've missed you so, Dane." The licking of his moist, hard tongue along her throat drew a shudder of desire.

"I can't believe the way you can destroy me." He lifted his head to frame her face in his hands, fingers curled into the just-washed fullness of her hair. "When I walked through that door I could have strangled you for the hell I'd been through." Weary lines were etched in his tanned skin, the strain of long hours leaving their mark. A gentleness glinted in his dark eyes as a half smile touched the corners of his mouth. "Do you know this is the first time I've seen you in a dress?"

"Is it?" she murmured absently because it didn't seem all that important to her.

"Of course, I've always been fully aware that you were all woman." He slid a hand down to cover her breast, letting its round contour fill his palm. "But it's an attractive sight to see you in a skirt just the same. Were you going somewhere?"

"Didn't Charlie tell you?" Pet couldn't seem to drag her eyes away from his mouth with its traces of her lipstick. Those strong male lips could create such an upheaval in her senses. "We were going to have a sandwich together."

"He's married," Dane stated.

"Yes. He's just a friend," she explained in case he wondered. "I didn't want to eat alone." Hope leaped with an eternal flame. "Are you free? I can tell Charlie —" But Dane was already shaking his head.

"No, I'm tied up this evening." He didn't volunteer any specific information as to whom he would be with or why he was wearing an evening suit and tie. "I wanted to be certain you'd arrived safely. I expected you an hour ago."

"Charlie doesn't drive as fast as you do," Pet smiled, and tried not to wonder about his plans for the evening.

His light kiss seemed to be a reward for not asking. "I want you to have dinner with me tomorrow evening, after the taping is finished. No one else. Just the two of us," he invited.

"I accept." She let her lips tease his. "On condition that you don't take me where I need to dress. This is all I brought."

"On the contrary." Dane returned the torment, rubbing his lips against hers while his fingers found her nipple beneath the bodice of her dress and teased it into erectness. "I'll take you somewhere that you have to *un*dress."

"You would!" Pet accused.

"You bet." His mouth closed on hers, parting her lips to drink in her sweetness.

A knock at the door brought the kiss to a lingering end. "It's probably Charlie," she whispered against his mouth.

Reluctantly Dane let her go. "You'd better answer it. I have to leave anyway."

Pet moved unwillingly out of his arms to walk to the door. Remembering, she half turned to warn him, "You have lipstick on your mouth."

When she opened the door, Charlie had

brought Lon Baxter with him. "I bumped into Lon in the elevator, so I invited him to join us if that's all right," he explained, and glanced past her to see Dane. "Hello."

Pet glanced over her shoulder to see Dane returning his handkerchief to the inside pocket of his suit jacket. She supposed the two men would reach the obvious conclusion as to why he had needed to wipe his mouth. She would have been less than honest if she didn't admit she was a little self-conscious.

"Hello, Charlie, Lon." Dane nodded to both men, but his gaze narrowed dangerously on the latter. Then he was moving alongside her, touching her shoulder lightly in farewell and smiling. "I'll see you tomorrow." An oblique reference to their dinner engagement.

"Tomorrow," she promised, saying more with her eyes.

The two men stepped to one side to let Dane pass, then Charlie raised a questioning eyebrow. "Ready?"

"Just let me get my bag," Pet nodded, and went to retrieve it from the dresser.

Nothing was said initially about Dane's being in her room, although Lon's gaze was often half-angry when it met hers. The conversation during their meal centered on the production, with Lon filling them in on what had gone on here while they were in Batsto. After the waitress had cleared their plates and served coffee, Pet took a cigarette from her pack and bent her head to the match flame Lon offered.

"Dane sounded worried when you didn't answer your phone." Charlie finally brought up the subject that had occupied both men's minds. "Where were you?"

"Taking a shower." She didn't go into the circumstances of the other times.

"You're making a fool of yourself, Pet," Lon said irritably. "All he wants is to take you to bed."

"That's the pot calling the kettle black, isn't it?" Pet challenged, releasing a thin stream of smoke and tapping the end of the cigarette in the ashtray.

"Maybe it is." Lon reddened, but he wasn't deterred. "But it doesn't change the facts."

"And those facts are?" Her voice was as cool as her glance.

"The only way there's a future in having an affair with him is if you're sleeping with him to get some promotion in the company. Even then, I wouldn't be too sure that you wouldn't be out of a job when the affair ends. Why would somebody like Dane Kingston want an old lover working for him?" He leaned forward to stress his arguments.

"I haven't slept with him, and I'm not becoming involved with him because I want a promotion, a raise or anything like that," Pet denied, and sipped at her hot coffee, trying to appear indifferent even though Lou's blunt appraisal of her motive had stung.

"Then the only thing you're going to get out of this affair is a lot of painful memories and regret, because it isn't going to last," he insisted.

"Why won't it?" she challenged.

"Leave it alone, Lon," Charlie urged. "It's none of our business."

But Lon ignored him. "He's Dane Kingston and you're Petra Wallis, that's why it won't last. You may be a beautiful woman, but his world is one long string of beautiful women. You can't compete with the glamour and excitement of the likes of Ruby Gale. Maybe he's through with her now, but there'll be someone else like her down the line. What are you — little Pet Wallis — going to do then?"

He shook his head as if despairing that he could get through to her. But he was. Everything he was saying was being driven into her like a nail in a coffin. "If you want an affair, have it with an average guy like me. If not with me, then with someone like me. At least you'd stand a chance to have something that might last."

"I appreciate the advice," she said stiffly.

He sighed. "I know you aren't going to believe this, coming from me, but I like you, Pet. I don't want to see you get hurt."

"I like you, too, Lon," was the only reply she could make.

It was hectic getting ready for the last taping.

Because another performer had given his show the night before they weren't able to set up the bulk of their equipment until the day of the taping. An hour before show time, Pet was helping Andy secure a cable that had worked loose from the adhesive strip taping it to the floor.

"Hey, Pet!" Rick called to her from the stage and motioned. "Dane wants to talk to you."

"Tell him I'll have a headset on in a few minutes."

"No. He's backstage," Rick explained.

Andy glanced at her. "Go see what he wants. I'll finish up here."

Wiping her moist palms on the hips of her brown slacks, Pet left him — but none too eagerly. Yesterday she would have raced for the chance to speak to Dane. But Lon's warning had forced her to take a long, hard look at where she was going. She didn't question anything Dane had told her or his desire for her. It was the things there hadn't been time to say — things she wasn't even sure he would have said if there had been the time. She was getting nervous about having dinner with him after the show because she knew where it would lead, and she wasn't sure anymore if that was where she wanted to go.

Backstage it was becoming a confusion of singers, dancers and stagehands arriving and mixing with the production crew. Pet hesitated, glancing around for the familiar sight of Dane's tall muscular frame. But she didn't see him. Instinct guided her in the direction of Ruby Gale's private dressing room.

He was standing outside the door, half-turned away from her. Pet stopped when she glimpsed the red-haired woman with him. She didn't want to approach him while he was with Ruby and possibly arouse the star's temper by her presence. Since neither of them had noticed her in the midst of all the people, Pet stayed where she was until he was finished.

In a punishing kind of fascination, she noticed the way Dane's hands rested on Ruby's hips with such familiar ease. Her fingers were playing with his shirt-front and running through the curling collection of exposed chest hairs. Something plummeted to the pit of Pet's stomach when she realized her hearing had become attuned to their voices.

"Darling, I feel so badly about tonight," Ruby was saying. "We've planned for so long to celebrate with champagne and caviar, and now I can't make it."

She couldn't make it? Pet had thought the date was off because Dane had canceled to have dinner with her. No, she wasn't going to think of herself as a substitute. Dane had said he and Ruby were finished, so what did it matter?

"Naturally I'm disappointed," Dane replied, and didn't mention anything about having another engagement. It wasn't necessary that he should. "I shouldn't be celebrating now anyway. My work is just beginning, editing it all together into a smooth, fast-paced show. It's just as well that we have to postpone it."

"You're always so understanding, Dane." Ruby beamed and stretched on her toes to kiss him.

"I understand that the star has a show to get ready for and she's letting me detain her." The kiss he gave back was little more than a peck. He turned her around and gave her a gentle push toward her door. "Go and make yourself beautiful."

With a husky laugh, Ruby Gale slipped into her dressing room. As Dane turned to leave, his gaze immediately fell on Pet. She started forward quickly, so he wouldn't guess she had been standing there watching and waiting, a bright smile fixed on her expression. His features gentled at her approach.

"Rick said you wanted to talk to me," she explained.

"All the time . . . about the silken texture of your hair, the softness of your lips, the heady warmth of your body against mine," he murmured, caressing her with his voice and his velvet dark eyes. Then he seemed to catch himself and took a deep, regretful breath. It was strange, because Pet couldn't breathe at all. "But on this occasion it was business. I want you to get some behind-the-scenes action before the show starts — dressing rooms, makeup, wardrobe, musicians, stagehands. You know the kind of color I want. And concentrate on what goes on in the wings during a performance. You should be able to pick up some audience shots in the background."

"Sure." Pet continued to stand there, looking at him, loving him, and struggling to display the professionalism of her craft.

"Then you'd better get a move on," Dane urged with a dancing look, "before I take you behind that curtain and make love to you."

Her pulse went to pieces, losing any semblance of normality. Behind that glint of amusement in his dark eyes a desirous light burned.

"Yes, sir." Breathless, she mocked a formal salute and turned to hurry away.

By the time she had got the hand-held camera, strapped on all its paraphernalia and commandeered a helper named Tom to carry the recorder and keep the attached wires and cords out of the way, it was half an hour before show time and preparations for the performance were in full swing backstage. She noticed Dane standing on center stage in consultation with her three co-workers who would be manning the cameras out front. They were going over his detailed notes on each number.

Her gaze lingered on his lithely brawny build for an aching second, but her task had already been assigned, so she set to work to begin fulfilling it with Tom tagging along after her like a faithful dog carrying its master's newspaper; only in this case he carried the recorder.

As she was setting up to get a shot of the general hubbub around the dressing rooms, a florist arrived with a huge standing bouquet of bloodred roses. Pet quickly seized on this piece of glamorous backstage color and followed him to the star's dressing room, the tape rolling.

Pet was standing some ten feet away when the door opened at the florist's knock. Luck gave her the perfect angle over the shoulder of the florist into the dressing room.

Clancy, the secretary and girl Friday to Ruby Gale, answered the door. Beyond her, Ruby Gale was sitting in front of a mirror with her back to the camera and the door, dressed in a lavender robe. The mirror's reflection gave Pet a view of the star's face. If it had all been rehearsed, it couldn't have been more perfect.

Evidently the florist had added some flattering comment of his own to the delivery of the roses, because the red-haired entertainer half turned to give him one of her sexy smiles. Her blue gaze flickered past him to the camera and Pet. She was instantly livid, coming to her feet and storming out of her room in a volcanic fury as flaming as her hair.

"You snooping little bitch!" she screamed at Pet. "What are you doing sneaking about out here?"

"I'm sorry." Pet tried to apologize and

explain about the flowers, but her voice was drowned by the vicious abuse and accusations Ruby Gale hurled at her. She attempted to retreat, backing away, but she was relentlessly pursued. Too stunned by the vitriolic attack, Pet understood only half of the insults.

"What were you hoping — that I'd be half-naked so you could sell the tapes to some gutter magazine? I know how you got your job! How many men did you have to sleep with to get it? I know your kind! You're nothing but a tramp!" Ruby raged.

Pet's face was scarlet, aware that everyone backstage was witnessing this vile scene. "You aren't on this production because of your skill with the camera!" Ruby went on. "It's your skill in bed, keeping the rest of the crew happy while they're away from home! You're a —"

"What's going on here?" Dane's angry voice was the most wonderful sound Pet had ever heard. She turned as he came striding forward, relief cooling her hot cheeks.

"This blond slut was snooping outside my door!" His arrival did not abate the redhead's abusive tongue. "She —"

Pet interrupted quickly, "The florist delivered some roses and I was —"

"You were sneaking about trying to —"

"No more." Dane intervened to lay soothing hands on Ruby's shoulders, which trembled with the fury of her wrath. "I don't want you getting upset. I'll take care of it. You can leave it to me now."

Pet stared at him incredulously, shock giving way to indignation. She was aware of the calming effect he was having on the star, but she wasn't the least bit interested in whether Ruby was pacified.

"I won't have her sneaking around out here," the redhead insisted. Some of the venom had been removed from her tone although it remained imperious.

"I promise you she won't bother you anymore." He curved an arm around the lavender-covered shoulders and turned Ruby toward her dressing room. "Don't worry about it."

Tears scalded Pet's green eyes. She furiously blinked them away, turning to see Tom staring at her, wordless in profound sympathy. Stiff with righteous anger and raw pain, she couldn't respond to his look. She didn't need to communicate her desire to move away from the star's dressing room as Tom picked up the recorder to walk with her. Pride kept her shoulders squared and her head high, but she was trembling inside from Dane's abandonment of her. She was determined not to let it show how deeply she was hurt.

That resolve flew out of the window when Dane came in search of her a short few minutes later. A wall of stormy tears kept her from seeing him too clearly, but she had a blurred image of his tight-lipped countenance, which was all her temper needed.

"How could you let her talk to me like that?" Her angry voice scraped her throat to make the accusation hoarse. "How could you let her get away with it?"

"It's only twenty minutes before the show starts!" Dane flared. "What did you expect me to do? Try to defend you and have her do one of her exit scenes? Then where the hell would I be with all this equipment and crew and a half-finished special?"

"I don't care who she is or how important she is, nobody has a right to talk to anybody like that — not to me! Not to Tom! Not to anybody!" Pet retorted in a husky protest.

"And what about the show?" he challenged.

"Oh, God, yes. The show!" Her voice was breaking, cracking under the strain. "You said you'd sold your soul for it — and you were right. You'll get your show, Mr. Kingston. And I hope it keeps you happy, because I won't!"

"Of all the damned time and places to pick —" he began in exasperation.

"You'd better leave. You've got work to do before the show starts." She turned away from him, pretending to adjust something with the equipment while she choked on a sob. It was an eternity of seconds before she heard him walk away. She closed her eyes at the shattering pain in her chest.

"Are you all right?" Tom murmured anxiously.

"I'm fine," she sniffed, and wiped at her nose before lifting her chin. "We'll do his damned show." The decision created a strange detachment that permitted her to get through the taping of the performance, functioning mechanically, completely emotionless. From the wings she got a shot of Ruby Gale accepting the final ovation from the crowd, a heartily applauding audience in the background, and exiting to the opposite side of the stage to receive the congratulations of her personal entourage.

The minute it was over Pet set the camera down and began unstrapping all the gear. "Take care of this stuff for me, Tom," she said tightly, and started to walk away. "I'm leaving."

"But if Mr. Kingston —"

"Tell him he has his show . . . and he can't fire me, because I quit."

Chapter Eleven

Moonlight silvered the foamy caps of the waves rushing onto the sandy shore. Pet lifted her face to the ocean breeze, closing her eyes to the pain that hadn't found a release. Her hair had long ago been freed from its confining pins as if loose and falling free it would somehow allow the hurt to tumble from her. But it hadn't.

Turning parallel to the ocean, Pet began to walk again along the stretch of beach. To her left was the Boardwalk and its towering buildings and hotels etched in lights against the night sky. She didn't know how far she had walked since she had bolted from the casino theater to wander aimlessly up and down the quiet beach, avoiding the piers with their noisy rides and bright lights. She wasn't the only one walking along the oceanfront. A few others were strolling its expanses, mostly couples.

A wave came rushing in to lap the firmly packed sand near her feet, but she ignored its mild threat. Her gaze wandered ahead, studying the strip of glistening wet sand that marked the extent of the tide's encroachment onto the beach. The dark figure of a man was standing ten yards in front of her by the water's edge, but facing her and not the sea. Her heart gave a painful thump in her chest as she recognized Dane and paused.

Refusing to run or walk up to him, Pet took a few steps into the soft sand beyond the reach of the waves and sat down. Her hand shook as she lighted a cigarette and stared out to sea. Drawing her knees up, she rested her forearms on them. The sand crunched under Dane's approaching footsteps, but she didn't look up when he stopped beside her.

"I'd just about given up hope that I would find you." His voice was low and husky. "I looked everywhere — the hotel, the casino, up and down the Boardwalk. If it hadn't been for all that golden hair shining in the moonlight, I would probably have gone on looking all night for you."

Pet made no reply, not even acknowledging his presence with a look. She took another puff of the cigarette and watched the breeze blow the curling smoke away from the burning red tip. Inside she was dying.

"Don't you know you shouldn't be walking alone at night?" But when his question was met by her continued silence, Dane sighed heavily. "I can't even make you angry, can I?"

There was an agonizing tightness in her throat. The paralyzing numbness that had kept everything dammed up inside was wearing off. She started shaking and had to bury the cigarette in the sand to keep from dropping it.

"You were right, Pet," he said with a throbbing hoarseness. "I sold my soul for that show."

A tiny, agonized sound slipped through the constricted muscles of her throat.

He continued to tower motionless above her. "Pet, you're the only one who can buy it back for me."

The husky appeal in his voice finally pulled her head up. She searched his shadowed face. The pride and strength remained forever carved into his features, but his dark eyes were haunted.

"When the show was over and I found out you'd walked out, I didn't try to find you right away. I went back to the control van and sat there, going over in my mind what had happened and what you'd said." Turning, Dane sat down on the sand beside her, adopting her position and letting handfuls of sand run through his fingers. "I thought I had the thing that was most important to me right there in front of me — the show tapes. Not in so many words, but you told me what an arrogant, selfish bastard I was. I've been called that before, but coming from you. . . ." He sighed heavily and clasped his hands between his spread knees, studying his linked fingers. "What I'm trying to say, Pet, is that what's important to me is your love and respect. Nothing else means anything."

"You don't really mean that, Dane," she whispered sadly. "You just want me to forgive you so you'll feel better. You don't care whether or not I love you. We haven't even known each other long enough to fall in love."

"Maybe you haven't, but I've been waiting for you all my life." His gaze locked onto hers and refused to let it go. "I love you, Pet. I realized it the morning that I came into your room to wake you up, and I knew that I wanted to wake you up every morning for the rest of my life. It was too soon. I couldn't tell you then. You would have thought I was handing you some line to persuade you to sleep with me. So I waited, knowing you were attracted to me and hoping that after this show was finished I'd have the time to make you fall in love with me, too."

"You don't even know me." She shook her head for a moment, breaking the spell he was casting.

"I know you. After our run-in a year ago, I made it my business to know about you. At the time I told myself my interest was purely professional," he said with a humorless laugh. "I personally reviewed everything you did, every project you were on, your past employment, your education, your family, everything. If you weren't any good, I was going to get rid of you — this green-eyed blond who told me to shut up."

"You've finally got rid of me. I quit." She wouldn't let herself be swayed by his revelations. He had hurt her too deeply tonight. It wasn't something that could be easily forgiven or forgotten.

"Pet, I erased the show tapes — all of them."

"What?" She jerked around to stare at him, wary and frowning.

"It wasn't an impulse. I thought it over very hard before I did it. You can call it a noble gesture if you want, but it was the only way I could prove that you were more important to me than the special."

"You shouldn't have done that!" She was stunned, incredulous.

"Why not?" Now he was watching her, his gaze searching through every nuance of her expressions.

"Because . . . all that work . . . all that time. . . ." It was impossible to think of all the reasons when there were so many. "You've spent a lot of money."

"A lot of money," Dane agreed. "But it's worth every dime if you finally believe me."

"I believe you." After that kind of sacrifice, how could she doubt him?

"Do you forgive me?"

"Of course," Pet breathed, just beginning to realize the fulfillment this meant. "Dane, I fell in love with you, too. I was the most wretched person in the world when I thought the man I loved could care so little about me that —"

But she was never allowed to complete the sentence as his hand reached to pull her off balance and into his arms. He was kissing her and murmuring love words that she would cherish in her heart forever.

When Dane finally allowed her to surface

from his loving assault, she was lying on the sand, her head pillowed on his sinewy forearm while he leaned partially over her. She drank in the sight of his compelling face above hers, passionately ardent in its expression.

"When will you marry me?" he demanded.

An old fear returned. "Do you really think I can keep you happy?" she whispered with a catch in her voice.

"No one else can. Haven't you accepted that yet?" he mocked. "No one else can irritate me and goad me into an argument quicker than you can. No one else can touch me and make my senses swim with desire. From no one else do I demand such perfection as I do from you. You make me happy with a smile."

"Ruby Gale —" Pet began.

His mouth thinned in grimness. "Once and for all, let me exorcise that devil from us. It was always business between Ruby and me. The physical side of our relationship developed out of it because we were members of the opposite sex. She had sexual needs and so did I. Emotions were never involved on either side. I can't say that I'm particularly proud of it, but she's a stunning and sexual creature, and I am just a man."

"That's just it, Dane," she tried to explain again. "In your business there will always be women like Ruby Gale."

"God forbid!" he muttered.

"Please, I'm serious," Pet insisted.

"But none of them will be you. Can't I get it through your head that I love you? It isn't just desire or physical gratification. It's love."

His mouth closed onto hers to convince her of the difference. Pet became quite enchanted with his efforts as his weight pressed her onto the soft bed of sand. She was breathless and starstruck when he finally transferred his attention to the hollow of her throat. She splayed her fingers through his dark hair, quivering as his hands worked deftly at the buttons on her blouse.

"Do you think this is a proper behavior for a lady?" she whispered with a trace of teasing amusement. "Letting a man make love to her on a public beach? After all your lectures, Dane Kingston, what will people think if they see me?"

"Dammit, Pet!" He started to get angry, then laughed. "I have champagne chilling in my room." He kissed her hard. "And if you dare say a lady wouldn't go to a man's hotel room, I'll strangle you!"

She linked her fingers around his neck and gazed at him impishly. "Who ever said I was a lady?"

We hope you have enjoyed this Large Print book. Other G.K. Hall & Co. or Chivers Press Large Print books are available at your library or directly from the publishers.

For more information about current and up-coming titles, please call or write, without obligation, to:

G.K. Hall & Co.
295 Kennedy Memorial Drive
Waterville, ME 04901
Tel. (800) 223-1244
Tel. (800) 223-6121

OR

Chivers Press Limited
Windsor Bridge Road
Bath BA2 3AX
England
Tel. (0225) 335336

All our Large Print titles are designed for easy reading, and all our books are made to last.